DARK NATION

Richard Chandler

VANTAGE PRESS
New York

This is a work of fiction. Any similarity between the names
and characters in this book and any real persons,
living or dead, is purely coincidental.

Cover design by KISKIS DESIGN

FIRST EDITION

Published by Vantage Press, Inc.
419 Park Ave. South, New York, NY 10016

Manufactured in the United States of America
ISBN: 0-533-15309-3

Library of Congress Catalog Card No.: 2005907055

0 9 8 7 6 5 4 3 2 1

To my grandparents, Nunzio and Mary.
Thank you for believing in me.

Part One

The American Dream

1

Manfred's Plot

"I want you to ask yourself a question for me. Why does the bad guy always have to lose? Have you ever asked yourself that question before? Every single piece of modern literature, every movie, every single play, short story, everything . . . Jesus Christ, I've seen an eight-millimeter pornographic film where the bad guy lost. Look at this world! It's coming undone. The screws are loose, and yet, the bad guy still always manages to be foiled. Why?"

The question lingered in the stale air like a cloud of dirty exhaust from a broken-down car.

"I really don't know. Let's just call it tradition," Marlana mumbled.

A cold sweat overtook her body. She was beginning to fear the situation. Things were taking shape in the favor of her aggressor. As usual, he was plotting something. His schemes were relatively simplistic, yet they always managed to throw a monkey wrench into the life of Marlana.

"What a poor answer. Look at you. You're as nervous as hell! Calm down, I'm not planning to hurt you if I don't have to. You know, sometimes the bad guy makes more sense than the good guy does. The villain always has a justification for his actions. The hero only wishes to save the day. But why? What is he getting out of it? In reality, probably nothing. This isn't that society where they used to make movies. If you defeat me now, you don't get the girl, you don't get any money, and you just leave thinking you did the right thing. But did you? Do the right thing?"

"I'd do anything to shut you up!" Marlana exclaimed; the whole time biting her bottom lip out of a nervous habit.

"I'm not going to stop this until you give me a good answer. Like I said before, the bad guy often has a justification for what he's doing. Sometimes, he's not as bad as one may think. Sometimes. Maybe he's just taking matters into his own hands and is doing what he thinks is right. Now if he's doing what he thinks is the right thing to do, then isn't he the same as the good guy?" the man asking the question pondered.

He raised a mug to his mouth and took a long hard slug of beer.

"Listen, Manfred, I've sort of known you for a long time. I don't like you. You are nothing but a scared little boy. You want others to feel the same way you do about the world. It's not going to happen. Why? Because you are wrong. Do you really believe no one's really good, and no one's really bad?" asked Jacob.

"Did my favorite hero just open his mouth? That's my point. That's why I want you and Marlana to join me. Forget about what we've done to each other in the past and let's be allies! Come on, damn it! It'll be fun!" Manfred begged the two.

He was all alone standing in a dark bar with two people he hadn't spoken to in over a year. Manfred peered down at his beer, which was almost consumed. He slowly swaggered over to the bar area and refilled his mug via the beer tap.

"I'm really a martini guy but the Council banned hard alcohol. I'm sure you knew that though."

"No, Manfred. I personally don't like you either," Marlana finally spoke forth after a few seconds' pause.

"Wait, what comment were you saying 'no' to? Oh, my invitation to join me . . . Why? Have you ever asked yourself that question? You think I'm a bad guy, that's why! Well, I tried to explain my position. If you don't want to listen, then we'll have to remain enemies. I'm misunderstood here; it's not fair," explained Manfred.

There was no one else in the bar. Just three people. Manfred reached into his dark overcoat. His hand slowly wrapped around the handle of a small silver .22 caliber pistol. It was his weapon of choice. As he gripped the handle tighter he thought about what he was about to do, and got an idea. He assumed that both Marlana and Jacob were in possession of weapons and they were on to him. Manfred had to change his tactic.

"I'm going to kill myself, then. If you don't come with me, then I'm going to take my own life," stated Manfred as he removed the firearm from his coat.

He raised the gun to his head and was supposedly about to pull the trigger, but froze.

"Wait, I know we're enemies, but we are not currently fighting. There's no need for this," stressed Marlana.

"You're going to have to take this gun away from me then."

Marlana approached Manfred and slowly took the weapon.

"Come on. You're being ridiculous! He's going to pull a fast one!" Jacob warned his girlfriend.

"No shit! Too late!" Manfred exclaimed, expressing a sick smile as he pulled Marlana's body up against his, spilling beer all over her.

He pressed the gun to her temple, and placed his index finger inside the trigger guard. He rested his head against hers.

"Oh, this feels so good. If only things were always this intimate between us."

"Just shoot him! Jacob!"

Marlana would have rather seen Manfred with a bullet in him than to be safe herself. Her intense hatred for the man in black had returned.

Jacob had removed a handgun of his own from under his jacket and aimed to kill. He just couldn't pull the trigger. If he somehow proved to be inaccurate, he could potentially hurt Marlana. Jacob wasn't going to take the chance of killing the woman he loved.

"This is so touching, and that is why the bad guy can win after all. He's always smarter and so much more devious than you are! You and your stupid emotions! Ha! I'm going to leave now with her, and you're not going to try anything stupid or I'll kill her," Manfred boasted.

His plan had so far worked.

"It's moments like this that make me feel so warm and fuzzy inside."

Manfred tilted his mug to Marlana's mouth, forcing her to have a drink. The back door swiftly opened and a man around forty had made his way inside. He wore brown leather pants and a red plaid shirt much like a Canadian lumberjack. Manfred, with his back turned, did not realize the man had entered. One blow struck Manfred directly in the center of his spinal column, causing him to scream in pain. He released his grasp on Marlana, and his firearm then hit the ground with a clink. The sudden noise of shattering glass echoed in the nearly empty bar. Marlana began to run to the open arms of her boyfriend but was intercepted by the man who had just drilled Manfred.

"Marlana Von. You're coming with me," the man spoke with an authoritative voice. "This is important. It's for your own safety," he said, grabbing her shoulders with his large baseball glove-like hands.

"You throw quite a punch, my friend. We don't want any trouble at all. Just let her go," Jacob begged the man.

The lumberjack, still holding Marlana with one giant hand, lifted the bottom of his shirt to reveal the symbol of the Union that was etched into his belt. It was painted red, white, and blue, and in the center there was some sort of a bird that Jacob had never physically seen before. He just knew what the symbol stood for.

"What? You should have said you were from the Union. As long as you don't hurt her, we'll go peacefully."

"What crap! Three on one! How typical. Why is it always me versus the world? Look at his belt, he's in the Union. You are part of the Union as well, Jacob, you moron, and yet he's kidnapping your girlfriend. You are far too trusting."

Manfred rose to his feet, glaring at his attacker. He possessed a white beard that helped hide his emotions. It was hard to tell if he was friend or foe. Manfred ran his fingers through his black hair and froze.

"Holy shit. You're here because you're her father. Her father who's saving her from the likes of me. Shit, it's like a cheap soap opera."

Manfred retrieved his weapon and headed for the door.

"Thank God he's gone. I'm so sick of that guy. Yet, there's something about him that I just can't put my finger on. He's hurt in some way," Marlana explained to the two men.

"Yeah, he's hurt alright. He'll be dead if he ever decides to pull a stunt like that again. I don't like him and the corrupt Empire he works for," her father said.

"There's a Union camp through the woods a few miles from here. Why don't we go there and we can talk? Oh, and you must be Jacob. I've heard about you before."

"Sir, it's an honor to finally meet you in person. I'm so sorry—I had no idea it was you when you first entered the room. How did you know where to find us?" he asked.

"I came for my daughter and didn't recognize you either, my boy. We have some catching up to do, but first we must talk about something. There's a reason why I needed to contact you two so abruptly. I fear we are about to see some really bad things happen if we don't do something fast."

"What kind of bad things?" Marlana questioned her father.

"It's not safe to talk about it here. Let's head to the camp."

He turned and began to walk out the door, followed by his daughter and her boyfriend, Jacob. Marlana's father opened the door and gasped in horror. He froze in terror, unable to speak.

"What's wrong?" Marlana asked only to gasp for air herself. *They* were here.

"Four members of the Council are making an appearance in a small town like this?"

"What in the hell do they want?" Jacob whispered, gazing at his girlfriend in disbelief.

"This is the very bad thing I was planning on telling you about."

Marlana's father knew why *they* were here. Something was wrong and they had come to fix it. Somewhere along the way, someone crossed the line. A rule of The Game had been broken and that always meant a lot of pain and suffering for everyone.

"There's always someone trying to ruin things for me. The Council is here? What the hell do they want? Someone must be playing dirty again."

Manfred was back. He hadn't gone anywhere; he had been waiting outside the bar the whole time.

"I would shoot you all right here, but I don't want to cause any commotion."

"Manfred, you're all alone. Now, go home and leave us," Marlana instructed as if she was reprimanding a naughty child.

"You think you can tell me what to do?" he asked, angrily. "I came here to ask if you'd join me and instead you tell me to leave!" Manfred carried on. "To make matters worse, members of the Council show up, and you know what that usually means."

"Why don't you go bitch to someone that cares," Jacob piped in.

Manfred's blood boiled. He was beginning to remember the past. For some reason whenever he grew angry enough, he suddenly recalled every ill word and deed he had ever received. The first one that came to mind was something that involved Jacob himself. Manfred stared at Marlana. He was gawking openly in front of everyone.

"What are you looking at?" she questioned.

"You, apparently."

Manfred had remembered something deep. Something that

used to generate restless nights back two or three years ago. Something that caused his soul to itch and only one thing ever seemed to scratch it.

"Whenever you used to talk to me, even if you were threatening me, it just really filled me up with hope. Hope that someday, we could actually get together."

"What the fuck? I can't believe you just had to remind me that you even attempted to date Marlana! I put a stop to that when a real man asked her out. That'd be me, by the way, Manny. Me," Jacob grabbed Manfred's black jacket by the collar. He bent the leather forward and pulled Manfred closer to his face.

"Do you understand that statement?"

"Wait, you two are still going out? I forgot. And to think I was just about to propose! Just kidding. I only do that once in a lifetime. The last time you and the Union murdered my bride-to-be. You just didn't kill her; you did it at our wedding! And for what, to kill some fat Imperial officer whom I barely knew!" snapped Manfred as he pushed Jacob off of him. "If you ever touch me again, I'm going to take your ass out. I was anyway, but now, I'm going to make sure I get the job done."

Jacob stared at Manfred in disbelief for a good twenty seconds. He wasn't sure what the right thing to do was. He wanted to tear him down right there but it was a public place. The rules of The Game banned fighting between the Union and Empire in public places. He thought about it for a second. Jacob raised his right arm and was about to strike Manfred regardless, when a member of the Council interrupted him. He clutched Jacob's forearm and immediately stared him down. Jacob suddenly forgot all about Manfred and feared for his life.

"There are rules. You just broke one of the most important rules of them all," the Council member spoke in a harsh dry voice.

He wore a plain black robe and had long red hair tied in a ponytail. They all looked the same; every single one of them. In all the years Jacob had been in the Union he had never seen a member of the Council that looked different than any of the other ones. The Council itself was the undisputed national power system that controlled the entire country and one third of the rest of the known world. They were the ones responsible for the ongoing war between the Empire and Union. It was obvious to anyone; the sole reason that they continued the war was to facilitate their complete domination. The citizens of this country were too preoccupied fighting among themselves to bond together and bring down the Council's unfair rule. It was a well-oiled machine that ran in total secrecy. No one knew who the leader was. No one dares to find out. If any of the rules of the war, also known as "The Game," are broken, the Council always finds out about it. When they do, anyone from either side is dealt with accordingly.

"I'm sorry. It won't happen again. We'll leave this town," Jacob attempted to explain.

Now, everyone knew that fighting does occur in public. Whole towns had been destroyed as a result. They changed the rules as they went along and that was the big problem. One could never be sure if they were breaking the law or not. *How would you know?* The Council relied on people that didn't ask questions. That's how they survived without revolution.

"You're coming with us," the Council member stated, never taking his eyes off of Jacob.

"No, please, I beg of you! Let him go," Marlana pleaded.

She knew that anyone the Council arrested was never going to be seen again. There hadn't been a single case where someone was set free. Not even a rumor. She quickly grabbed Jacob's arm, trying desperately to hold on, before they completely seized him and began to drag him away. Jacob didn't resist much. He understood that there was no hope of escape. Maybe if he acted on his best behavior they'd kill him quickly. He stared at Marlana lovingly. A tear trickled down the side of her face. Both Marlana and Jacob's souls collapsed and the small amount of happiness they shared ceased to exist.

Manfred also came to the realization of what just took place. He thought he did a good job foreshadowing this scheme when he spoke of dating Marlana but no one seemed to notice. It was a setup played by Manfred all along. He lured Jacob outside, got him angry enough, and the rest was history. He removed a pack of smokes from his jacket pocket and slowly slid one out to celebrate his victory. Manfred first lit the cigarette, and then focused his attention back on the situation. *What a day!* In all the confusion no one looked back to see the sinister smile stretched across his face. He definitely gained something out of this, but in his mind, it wasn't the arrest of Jacob. Manfred casually glanced in the direction of Marlana with a devilish look in his eyes.

2

The Kidnapping

Marlana turned to her father and rested her body against his. She covered her face in his flannel shirt and began to cry. Manfred clutched the leather of his jacket just under the collar. He smiled in victory, all the while taking a prolonged gander at the now single Marlana.

"Listen, I'm sorry. If I even had an idea that this was going to happen I wouldn't have come," Manfred stated, breaking the silence after a full ten minutes.

Marlana did not acknowledge him. She continued weeping on her father's shoulder. Mr. Von just gazed down at the ground, praying that his daughter would be able to recover from this.

"It'll be okay. They'll free him after a week or so."

He tried to comfort her but she continued crying anyway. Marlana knew that Jacob was not going to be released from prison. They'd never let him go. Anyone that was taken away did not come back. The Council members had disappeared, returning to their normal routine of patrolling the town.

"I have official business in Boston this afternoon regarding the Empire," said Manfred.

He reached into his jacket and froze.

"I'd never go with you," Marlana muttered, barely able to speak after what she had just witnessed.

Her defenses were down.

"I didn't ask if you wanted to or not!" exclaimed Manfred, drawing a taser and stunning both Marlana and her father.

Their bodies hit the ground with unconditional force. A small line of blood trickled from the mouth of Mr. Von.

"You I need," Manfred uttered, smiling at Marlana. "And you, I don't need."

The .22 pistol once again made its triumphant return, this time finding its mark.

"Bye-bye, jackass."

A final gasp of air exited the lungs of Marlana's father.

"Number of heroes killed today . . . two and rising, baby."

3

The Game

The midnight express screeched its whistles and the train exited Quincy Station and headed for Boston. Marlana was beginning to regain consciousness. The world around her was slowly re-forming. Blackness brightened to color. Manfred was peering into the blankless of her eyes. Marlana wasn't entirely sure what had happened other than she was now the prisoner of the man that she hated most, and was well on her way to enemy territory.

"It doesn't have to be like this you know. I understand I can be a real asshole, but business is business, Marlana. I don't want this. I want you to be with me. I've always loved you. Jacob's gone forever. We can change this world, together . . . " Manfred trailed off.

It was hard for him to finally just come out and express himself to Marlana. He had made it obvious that he liked her in the past; however, not to this degree.

"You son of a bitch! I will never ever give myself to you in any way, shape, or form! Go to hell and rot there, you prick!"

Marlana definitely wasn't afraid to express herself. She knew it was Manfred's fault that Jacob was going to die. She'd never forgive him for this.

"But why? Can you answer that question? Answer it for me. I want to hear an answer. Don't tell me it was because of Jacob. That was the Council's doing, not mine," Manfred tried to explain himself.

He couldn't bear to look Marlana in the eyes any longer; a sudden of wave of tension rang throughout his body.

"You're in the Empire. I'm a Union girl. It just can't happen; you know that. I don't love you anyway. I don't even like you," Marlana stated.

She thought about Jacob, and what had happened to her father. She hadn't seen him since she woke up.

"Screw the Council. You do realize why they created a war between us, don't you?"

Manfred fixed his eyes on Marlana's shoes. A yearning burned in Manfred's forehead. He felt sick. There was only one cure for this sickness and it was Marlana herself. Manfred was not a complete man without her presence. Even in the midst of war, just being in the same place with her did something for him. A portion of his emptiness was filled. Whenever he was with her for whatever reason he always wanted to express his feelings for her, but he knew that was impossible. The rules of The Game made this impossible. His mind screamed for mercy, but he could never clear his head.

"The Council created The Game because they want us to fight and that's it. If we fight they can control the entire nation. No one has the time to fuck with them if they're preoccupied killing each other."

"People go along with it because there's no choice. I'm not stupid, Manfred, but I don't want to die for you. It's against the Council's law for us to be 'together' and you know that."

Marlana began to get up. She wasn't planning on escaping, just stretching. Manfred did seem to care for her and she thought he might end up freeing her when they arrived in Boston. Some of her tension suddenly disintegrated.

"Marlana, all my life I've felt uncared for. Don't let this feud created by the Council and all their bullshit control you. They are drones of the society they've created and nothing more. There are more of us than there are of them. The problem is that no one has the courage to stand alone and defy them. We're the real people, not them. I need you; I've never felt this way about a woman before. Defy the Council! You should have all the rea-

15

son to do so, they killed your father!"

Manfred was truthful in regard to all the words he had spoken, except for the last sentence, of course.

"What? Oh my God!"

Marlana was dazed from Manfred's bluntness.

"The Council will pay in time, I promise you that."

She began to cry. Tears once again ran down her pale face.

"Don't cry; it was definitely not your fault. Probably mine . . . they attacked me and him, but I escaped," Manfred lied. "Listen, why live in a world created by them? Don't you want to be free? I like doing things my way. The Council is small and we are large, yet they control us because we are at war. We should control them. There should be no social limitations put on anyone, especially by a few people."

Manfred meant what he said this time. He'd always hated social limitations. The thing he couldn't stomach about them was the fact that the ones calling the shots were always the few. *Who chose them in the first place?*

The ends justify the means, Manfred thought to himself.

In his mind this was the only way to bond with Marlana. He didn't want to have to kill her father but in his estimation there was nothing else he could have done.

Over the years Manfred had built up an overload of aggression. He started off with hope but was now left with a morbid nothingness. When he was a young boy, the other children always picked on him. All through his early life Manfred was excluded and looked down upon by his peers. He had always been different from the other children. They took exception to this and made his life miserable. Manfred could never understand why he was different. He wasn't a complete sociopath; he simply never found his place. All hope was lost as he continued living life this way. Wanting to love instead of constantly feeling bitter and depressed, he had discovered Marlana. She had served as his outlet for hope. There was only one problem: she was in the Union. Manfred joined the

Empire, however, and that pretty much ended that.

Things just weren't the same anymore. Nothing seemed right. Everything that occurred had a sinister motive to it. It was either you or them. There were always two sides to a story. The side that depicted someone as a hero and good, and the side that depicted him as evil. If one decided to look up the word "hope" in a modern dictionary, it wouldn't be listed. They had just stopped printing it, probably because people ceased to use it. New words had entered the English language; however, all synonyms for agony. There was nothing to put your faith into these days but alcohol. Bars and places where someone could get a drink were the only really successful businesses in downtown Boston.

Around thirty years ago the stock market had had a terrible crash. After years of peace, the United States suffered a string of terrorist attacks all issued by military factions from the east. Every major U.S. city was badly damaged. The fatalities were like nothing anyone had ever witnessed. All of the country's great corporations from businesses that created food products to weapons manufacturers, all closed their doors. There's nothing a country can do if millions of companies declared bankruptcy. The federal government paid the first wave of expenses to try and keep some of the major companies afloat. But there was just one fated crash after another and the government could no longer withstand the disaster. The president abdicated his power. His authority transferred to the next in line, the vice-president, naturally. That's where *everything* went wrong. Not just for the United States, but for the world.

The one fear of the free world finally came into reality. Not during the Cold War, but now, there was a nuclear holocaust. Close to eighty-five years after The Bay of Pigs Incident, it had finally happened. Tension between world leaders grew to epic proportions with each passing day.

A small country in West Africa fell to the Red Plague: Communism. It had wielded its triumphant return once again when the world was folding in on itself. People all around the world lacked money and resources, but especially in the Third World countries. Communism always seems to rear its ugly head whenever the world's citizens are deprived of their human rights. The free countries did not stop the spread of Communism either. Before long, the entire west coast of Africa succumbed, along with the former Russian territories. Not that the Russians and Africans got along well; however, one must recall that Russia still possessed a great deal of nuclear weapons. The new president of the United States felt it had become his duty to thwart the Red Plague by declaring war on Russia. A good lesson in life is to not engage with a group of people that have already hit rock bottom. The government had to resort to Communism, in an attempt to save its people, and it wasn't going to back down from the United States. Its economy was barely functioning, its people could care less if they went to war; life couldn't get any worse.

For a short time, both governments did better economically. The war had boosted production by close to sixty percent; until the first nuclear bomb was detonated in the United States. A terrorist, it was never confirmed if they were even working for the Russians or not, activated a bomb at the capital. The U.S. retaliated by launching several nuclear missiles on Russian soil, almost completely wiping it off the map. Radiation spread throughout the atmosphere and generated sickness. The government, once again, spent literally all its money on keeping its citizens alive.

The vice-president vanished one day, probably in fear of being assassinated, and the country was left leaderless. That is when all hell broke loose. Middle Eastern terrorist organizations formed an alliance with virtually all Third World countries. An anarchist from the east; referred to only as "Horace," rose from their ranks. They vowed to destroy the United States at all costs. This was not a new problem. Especially from terrorists of the Middle East, but this time they were a well-oiled machine. They functioned as a unit. The United States fought hard and well against the new enemy, but there were complications.

18

That's when *they* showed up. A nameless group of militants appeared, covering the United States. They were everywhere and claimed that they had the answers and could solve the country's problems. Due to political issues regarding the war, the country was in the process of splitting into two separate organizations that would deal with current affairs by their own means. People were hungry and in need of money desperately. *They* filled the position as leaders of the country, in its totality, with their preaching and false promises of good fortune. What became of the Constitution no one was certain. In fact, little was known from that point on what had happened, exactly. No records existed in regard to this segment of history. This nameless, leaderless organization totally replaced the government within months and, surprisingly, they did not do it by force. People were willing to try anything that could possibly lift the burden, so not a citizen bothered to fight back or to interfere. *They* had won, and from that point on, they were known as the Council. Every element of the old world had disintegrated. A new system of rules that everyone simply had to follow etched themselves into the heart of the country. If these rules were broken, punishment was always death. The people had oppressed the people.

Not a single soul was strong enough to challenge the Council. They were invincible. Most citizens conformed to them out of fear. No one questioned his or her own oppression. It had become part of everyday life. The war continued between the Alliance and the U.S., resulting in the detonation of more nuclear bombs in what was now left of America. The threat of total anarchy gave the Council the ability to control all forms of media and communication. No one was a private citizen any longer and for the time being no one cared—as long as they were protected. Due to a wall of radiation that encircled New England, the Council was forced to centralize its government within. It was futile to try to escape: heading west or south would result in death by radiation poisoning.

There was no written documentation on how or why it happened, but the Council had established The Game. There existed two sides that competed in the ongoing conflict: the Empire of Despair and the Union. They were the two largest tribal organizations after the War of the Old World. Most people simply chose the side that their parents had been fighting for, but there had been rumored cases of young adults being bribed by one side or the other, abandoning, even killing their parents for a high-ranking position in the army. The sides themselves were pretty evenly matched; however, the Empire had a serious technology bonus and of course, land advantages. The Empire was known as the Empire because before the Council gained control of the country, it was the country itself. It had extended from the top of continent all the way down to the sea. The Union, on the other hand, was less strict and it was said to be less stressful once joined. The Union apparently had been part of the Empire at one time and split off for one reason or another and the Council capitalized on the situation. Each institution functioned with a distinct form of government; however, no matter the case, the Council manipulated every aspect of life. The history behind this phenomenon was unclear and the truth had yet to be discovered.

The Empire and Union, overseen by the Council, had now been warring for over ten years. It was a Council mandate that both factions must fight—co-existence was not tolerated. Despite this, the Council never allowed one faction to completely dominate the other. Americans, if one could still be considered an American, didn't understand why, but everyone went along with The Game. Perhaps they did it because they had no choice. Maybe it is now part of the culture. No one questioned it.

What comes next? Where does the world go from here? Is recovery possible? Manfred wondered. Things looked hopeless. Nothing seemed to be able to break the cycle. A perpetual darkness had descended over the land.

Manfred sat quietly, occasionally glancing at Marlana out of the corner of his eye. He reflected on the country's past, his past, and what he could remember of Marlana's. Something burned inside of him. He was not satisfied. Nothing in his life was what he wanted it to be. The Council more or less controlled him. He was forced to participate in The Game. Marlana would probably never love him. Manfred hadn't even seen his old drinking buddies in years. There was nothing to look forward to. Too lost in his own thoughts and negative emotions, Manfred didn't notice what was transpiring right next to him.

"Manfred . . . look!"

Marlana clutched the sleeve of his jacket.

"I'm sorry, sir. I had no idea you were talking to me."

It was a member of the Council. *Long hair in ponytail. Black robe. It was definitely a Council member.* Two encounters in one day was way too much for anyone.

"The woman beside you has been identified as Marlana Von, a member of the Union. You are Manfred . . . " another Council member interrupted the tall dark figure.

"Arrest them both. Two citizens from opposite sides cannot co-exist in harmony. They cannot be seen together in public. It is illegal," he told the other member in a low droning voice.

"No, she's a prisoner of mine. I'm taking her to an Imperial lock-up," Manfred attempted to explain.

"No listening!"

Manfred didn't know what to do for the first time all day. He had no idea what to say, or how to even position his body. Any sudden movement could mean his arrest. The next three seconds seemed like thirty minutes. Sweat poured off of Manfred's forehead like a faucet and it all ran into his mouth. He felt dizzy. Experiencing the urge to vomit, Manfred placed his hand on his stomach. *Could he get out of this?* His breathing began to increase dramatically. They were going to bust him, he just knew it. They could sense fear like a shark can smell blood.

Without warning, the train made a sudden stop. The two

Council members looked at each other and then back at Manfred, trying to figure out what was going on. The escape hatch closest to Marlana blew off the hinges and soared like a flying saucer out the opposite side of the train, tearing directly through solid metal. Six men, all dressed in brown leather and wielding blank expressions, entered the train. The first man drew a shotgun out from under his trenchcoat, emptying buckshot into the Council members. The looks on their faces were priceless as their bodies hit the floor. Manfred thought, *I may never get to see the death of a Council member again for the rest of my life.*

The man with the shotgun and his comrades wore neither the symbol for the Union nor the Empire. They didn't appear to be foreigners either. *That can only mean one thing...*

"Damn it, Manfred, rogues! We're being robbed!" Marlana stared in disbelief as the men opened fire on the citizens.

4

The Forgotten

Three bodies turned to five in an instant. The blood of the newly deceased flowed down the aisle, ceasing at Marlana's shoes. Manfred's socks were already beginning to feel damp. The midnight express lay silent as chaos reigned in her interior. No one moved a muscle until the shooting had come to a halt. These men were rogues. They had no place in the Union or the Empire: most were criminals of sorts. They sure as hell didn't work for the Council. All territory occupied by them functioned as a buffer zone for the war. Manfred almost admired their drive for irregularity. But avoiding The Game always came at a price. *They don't wish to follow the system that ruined their lives,* he thought, *the system that stole what was once theirs, making them rogues in the first place.* He decided to kill them anyway.

"Stay put, Marlana. I'm going to end this before they reach us."

"They're fucking savages," Marlana stated in a whisper.

"True. They made their point, however. Now they expect everyone to give them their valuables so they can sell them in the black market. I have no valuables."

"Neither do I. Do these assholes take credit?"

"What the hell is credit?"

"Oh, I almost forgot. You're a member of the Empire. It's the way we pay for stuff in Union towns and cities."

"Oh, well, I wouldn't know. You know how we pay for stuff in the Empire? With paper money. Like the good old days, ya know? Like before the wars."

"I don't care about that. Just save our asses."

"Oh, now that you can get something out of it, you're going to talk to me like we're friends? I think, Marlana, that sometimes we have a failure to communicate."

"What the hell? I think you should just shut up and accept it. Considering you kidnapped me and all!"

"Yeah. That is true. But someday you'll see things my way. I'm not the real bad guy, despite popular belief."

"Then what the hell are you? I don't think you're here for my amusement."

Manfred was beginning to sidetrack himself. He thought of Marlana in *that* way again. *What was this?* Guilt ran through the veins of Manfred as he glanced at the frightened expression that was stretched across Marlana's face. He should tell her the truth about her father. *Why did I have to kill him?*

Well, he didn't have to, but he was accomplishing two things at once. He blamed it all on the Council, thus turning Marlana completely against them, and at the same time eliminating an enemy that worked for the Council. *Yes, it was true.* Imperial intelligence had assigned Manfred a very special project: kill Gregory Von. He just had no idea that the sorry bastard would find him. *Talk about an easy job.* Well, it was done and now there's one less Council sympathizer in the world. Manfred despised traitors, even if they did turn against the Union. He figured if you were going to turn your back on someone and be a snitch, at least do it in the favor of the Empire.

Marlana sure looks cute when she's scared, Manfred thought to himself. "Jesus Christ. All I can think about is you."

Manfred didn't intend to slip out loud like that. It was just one of those things that happen. It took him four full seconds to come to the realization that he did, indeed say it, with Marlana present, gawking right at him, no less. She did remark on his comment but Manfred literally didn't hear her response. He was too busy worrying about the repercussions.

"What the hell, son? Aren't you forgetting about something?"

It was one of the rogues.

"Yeah, things aren't always the way they seem, right? He was a spy for the Council."

He had done it twice in a mere thirty seconds.

"What you say to me, boy?"

What happened after that, well, no one really knew. Well, someone knew. The rogues knew. But Manfred and Marlana didn't because they were both knocked unconscious by one of the robbers. Manfred remained on the train until Imperial backup arrived and Marlana's whereabouts were now unknown.

5

The Chosen One

Jacob stared in disbelief. This was not what he expected. Blood ran from his nose, into his mouth. A bitter taste, forcing him to gag.

"What the hell is this?"

Once again he was struck down. His hands were tied behind his back, making it impossible for him to stop the bleeding.

"Do you have anything else to say?"

The Council was going to kill him. They were just doing this as a method of demoralization.

"Go to hell."

There was no way Jacob was going to give in to this. He was not planning on dying without dignity.

"You want to live with dignity, don't you?" one of the hooded men asked.

Were they reading his thoughts? Jacob's head felt as if it was going to burst open, spilling his brains all over the room. The walls were a whitish-yellow—the color of vomit. The air in the room was so stale that it had its own taste. There were no windows or any visible means of ventilation. Only a door. Three of *them* just stood by observing, waiting for a response.

"What's going on?"

He probably shouldn't have opened his month. Jacob suddenly remembered that he never looked behind him. After slightly tilting his head, his eyes slowly glanced over his shoulder to see a most disgusting sight. There was a machine with four straps on it. It was large enough to tie down a full-grown horse. A pasty white substance covered the ground, encircling the machine. Jacob had no desire to know what that was.

"It's cerebral fluid."

They were literally reading his thoughts.

"Don't worry, you're not going to die. We're not ready to kill you. You will now decide your future. You are privileged. You are a chosen one."

They were beginning to scare the shit out of him. He had never seen a Council member this close, never mind three of them, all talking of things he couldn't possibly understand.

"Join us now. You have the power to help us."

"I'd never join you . . . " Jacob mumbled.

They invited him to be part of the Council. *Jacob in the Council?* Just to make sure that they had heard him correctly, Jacob reiterated himself.

"I'd never join you."

"We knew you'd say that."

Jacob was once again struck by one of the members. A strange sensation came over him due to light-headedness. The sheer loss of blood was crippling.

"You have been selected as one chosen to follow in your father's footsteps. You must comply."

"What do you know about my father?"

Jacob's father had vanished when he was just a boy. It was believed that highway bandits had murdered him. No one knew for sure. One night he simply never returned home.

"What do you know about your father?"

These Council officers were slowly pulling Jacob apart, hitting every major soft spot he had.

"You believe Marlana Von to be the love of your life. We have cameras, sensors, microphones, everywhere. She's cheating on you as we speak. Just thought you'd want to know."

"Bullshit!"

Jacob wasn't planning on buying into this garbage. They were attempting to break him down and gain access into his brain. The door opened across the opposite side of the room, and another Council member came through. Something was different about this one. He was smiling.

"I am the leader of your conversion. The man chosen to make first contact with the chosen one. That's you, by the way. I know what you're thinking. I'm not like all the others."

This one even spoke differently. He wasn't a drone. Jacob never heard of any leadership positions existing within the Council.

"Since you want to play hardball with us, you're going to be sent to room 567."

The man turned toward the door and the others followed him. Jacob was left alone in the small white room. He felt nauseated. He felt confused. *Had Marlana betrayed him?* The face he so desperately yearned to see, the man that appeared to be the leader figure, was now out of view. *Who the hell was he?*

6

Imperial Base

Manfred felt euphoric as he gazed out a nearby window. There were a few children playing outside. He looked beyond them, admiring the small community built for the citizens of Boston. A green field was a rarity these days. One-third of the country's soil had been absorbed by poison. Nuclear fallout, the one thing Manfred believed he had no control over. People died daily from radiation sickness. For reasons that perplexed its citizens, Boston was never directly bombarded with nuclear weapons during the War of the Old World. Good portions of the suburbs had been turned into ghettos, where constant fighting between the Empire and Union took place. Boston, on the other hand, was the second largest Imperial stronghold. Manfred possessed a feeling of safety here. Suddenly his inner security melted and his mind became clouded with emotions. His eyes refocused on the children.

"They're so damn carefree. Wait till they grow and have to fight. There are so many different kinds of war. They'll soon experience what we've all been going through."

Manfred rested on an old rickety chair. He yearned for Marlana to be there with him, but no one had any idea what had become of her. The rogues took her away, apparently. She'd be raped, then killed. As Manfred came to that despicable conclusion he hoped it would in that order. All of his inner hatred returned. He simply wanted someone to be there with him. He didn't care who. Society, the war, his situation, all ate away at his mind. He had no desire to be in this state. He was sick and tired of always being alone. Bitterness and the envy of the people that received every-thing that they ever wanted plagued his consciousness. *Why couldn't he find someone to talk to?* There was a war out there, so he chose to fight it. The Council had created a great deal of his prob-lems, and he has vowed to destroy them. *It's not that simple though.* A job of that proportion could not be completed unless he could clear his head of confusion. Marlana was the answer to his lifelong puzzle that functioned as a crippling disease.

The wall monitor blinked on. A familiar face appeared, replacing the Imperial logo of a blackbird, its wings extended, pointing downward. Manfred never really cared for the symbol—it reminded him too much of the "flying eagle" of the Union.

"Manfred," a man around fifty-five bluntly stated.

For a few seconds he completely ignored the voice. He desired for someone to accompany him. He despised loneliness, and that is why he was bitter and full of hate. *If I recognize my problem, why can't I change it? Is Marlana the answer or just another failure wait-ing to happen?*

"Damn it, turn around!"

"Sir, I'm sorry. There's just a lot on my mind."

"Report your status, Agent Vega."

"Von is dead. I put a bullet through his brain."

"Excellent work, Manfred. We have a new assignment for you then."

"Yes, Captain?"

"There is a shipment of weapons being sold to terrorists from the east."

"Yeah? Who's the one on the other end of the transaction?"

"We don't know for sure, but intelligence believes they're our own."

"What?"

Manfred was shocked that citizens of the Empire, true Amer-icans, or so he thought, would sell arms to foreign terrorists.

"Yes, we have confirmed one of the thieves stole these

weapons from our storage facilities in Quincy. That information is classified. We believe this is all going down tonight at the harbor, and I want you to check it out," the captain ordered.

"Alone? Are you kidding me?"

Manfred had never received orders like this before. Something was up.

"Yes, but don't worry. Backup will be close by if anything goes wrong. All we want you to do is take pictures. There will be an official mission briefing back at this monitor later today. You will be summoned then. Good day."

His face disappeared and the Imperial logo had returned on the small screen. *It could be worse.* Manfred still qualified as a trained soldier and could be used as even more of a pawn and be forced to fight in the run-down, decrepit ghettos.

"Wait, sir!"

Manfred's original train of thought had returned. The captain came back on.

"Yes?"

"Sir, do you think it's wrong to use underhanded tactics to accomplish something you know will help yourself or others?"

Manfred had to ask someone after what had happened earlier today, not even taking the time to think of how odd it was that the captain somehow heard Manfred's last comment and returned on the screen.

"You're damn straight. Whatever works to eliminate problems whenever they come up."

He vanished once again. Manfred didn't favor that comment. Suspicious or not, he had a job to do. He should prepare for the mission. Perhaps he'd visit the colonel first. It was better than speaking to a monitor, and it had been a while since he last saw an old friend.

7

Whereabouts Unknown

She was surrounded by walls. Some were physical and the others; they were something more. They were not made of rock or of stone. Marlana wished she could just disappear. She lay on her back staring at the ceiling of her holding cell, memorizing the pattern of cracks and spiderwebs. Her once white blouse was now covered in black dust. What seemed like weeks, in reality were only a few hours. Time moved so slowly. She thought about her life. She was all alone now. Jacob had been taken prisoner, and he was most likely going to die. Her father . . . she'd never see him again. It had all happened so fast, and now she had all the time in the world to drown in her own sorrow.

"I'm next," croaked a woman cloaked in a green shroud.

She had to really strain herself in order for those few words to exit her mouth. Marlana originally thought this woman to be a manikin of some kind, lying there on the filthy floor of the cell. Realizing that the woman was alive, Marlana decided to talk to her.

"Next?"

It was the only logical thing to ask. Marlana leaned forward, examining the bizarre woman. She was around thirty years of age and had dried-out blonde hair. Her clothing was made from cheap cloth that exposed her bare arms and legs. A tattoo of some sort decorated her right shoulder. *A red circle?* Marlana then experienced a sudden numbness in her arm. She quickly rolled up her sleeve and to her dismay; she too, had one of those red tattoos.

"You're going to be sucked dry, little girl," the woman said, her voice slowly beginning to fade.

"What the hell? Tell me what's going on here, right now!"

Marlana wasn't kidding either. She had always had the intent to keep herself mark free.

"You're going to die," the woman's voice once again trailed off. "They like me . . . they love me . . . but you're going to die."

She rested her head against the cold damp cell wall. A disturbing smile appeared on her pale face.

Two men approached the holding cell. Their faces held no expression. These weren't the rogues that had originally kidnapped Marlana. They were still at large somewhere.

"It's time. Get up," one of the men instructed as he opened the gate.

The woman in green slowly rose to her feet and walked over to the man that did not speak. She gazed at him lovingly.

"I want you today."

She placed her arms around his neck and pressed her body tightly against his. Marlana still didn't understand what was going on here. This was the most outlandish ordeal she had ever witnessed.

"The new one is good. Those traders have high standards. I'm sure we'll get a lot of money for her. I'd like to try out the inventory once or twice before we sell," one of the men commented.

Marlana's heart nearly burst open in her chest. *They were going to rape her, then sell her on the black market? This couldn't be happening.* Marlana could not envision herself as someone's property for the rest of her life. She searched frantically around the small cell for some sort of weapon to kill herself with. There was nothing. Agony had once again crept up behind her. This was it; her life was now a complete nightmare.

"Where am I?"

"Did I give you permission to talk?" the second man asked with authority.

"No, but I will talk if I damn well please!"

33

Marlana had had enough shit in one day to fill Boston Harbor. She wasn't going to stand back and be raped by two barbarians.

"I respect your desire to be set free, but you can't blame us for this. A man that claimed to be your ex-boyfriend came by. We offered you to him, for a price of course, and he refused."

"That's impossible! He'd never . . . what was his name?" Marlana surely had no intent for such pessimism, but she knew she'd never see Jacob again.

"Jacob of the Union."

"And how much did Manfred pay you assholes to say that?"

No word in the English language existed to describe Marlana's rage.

"No. His name was Jacob. Blond hair. Around six foot one. He refused to pay for you. He said you abandoned him and weren't worth the money," the man that was holding the strange woman explained.

Marlana once again glanced around the room for something to kill herself with. Nothing. *Jacob . . . could he have betrayed me?* So many emotions tore through Marlana. Mistrust. Pain. Sorrow. Agony.

"Hon, it's not so bad. You'll learn to love these boys like I did," the shrouded woman remarked and lifted up her garment to expose more of her pale thigh. She ran her hand up her leg and froze at her crotch. Licking her lips, she looked back at the man she had been caressing.

"Shut up, whore."

Marlana was not going to give in to this.

"Don't worry, man, we'll sell this one at the underground fair tomorrow instead of next week, if she doesn't cooperate."

"Why do I have this tattoo?"

Marlana lifted her sleeve, revealing the crude circle of red.

"That's a secret. You'll find out soon enough," he smiled and turned to his friend. They casually walked out of the cell, locked it back up, and disappeared. The whorish woman attempted to follow them; however, the gate had been slammed in her face.

"No! I was so close. They haven't had sex with me in nearly three days," she complained talking directly to Marlana.

She began to walk slowly in her direction. When she finally reached Marlana she clasped her hands around her waist and pulled her up against her body.

"Why don't you say we . . . "

The woman was cut off by a fist full of rage, dropping her to the floor. She gazed up at Marlana and smiled, although she was in pain. Her garment had fallen back all the way and completely exposed her pasty white legs. She placed her left foot on Marlana's stomach all the while never removing that smile from her face. Marlana closed her eyes and bent down nearly on top of the woman. Filled with joy, the woman in green thrust her legs around Marlana's waist and reached upward for her breasts. Marlana gave her a look as if she was interested and smiled as fist after fist tore the woman's face apart. She did not stop until the whore's face was completely covered in blood and she lay silent underneath Marlana. That deranged smile had never faded.

8

Room 567

There was no difference between Room 567 and the one that Jacob had been in previously. He didn't care about these interrogation chambers. He wanted to see the core of the Council. There were so many unanswered questions. Jacob yearned to discover the truth. *Where did they come from? They seemed to just appear out of nowhere. What did they really do to rid the U.S. of its previous government? The citizens are led to believe no violence was used and the Council was doing everyone a favor by replacing democracy with totalitarian socialism, both the Empire and Union contributing to its greater good. Some favor! And the most important question . . . who is behind all of this? It can't be just another man in a hood. He has to be real.* If he were going to die, he'd at least be content learning this information. Jacob's face suddenly grew sensationally cold. Dizziness, directly followed by a sudden wave of nausea, caused him to collapse onto the milky-white floor. The walls were barren, and everything was the usual color of white.

There is no difference between this room and the others, Jacob thought to himself.

For no apparent reason Jacob suddenly felt the urge to touch his face. It wasn't just an urge; it had to be done. At first, he resisted. They were somehow reading his thoughts. He wasn't going to fall for these games of theirs. Tears rolled freely down his face. His left eyebrow twitched uncontrollably. He vomited but it didn't hit the floor. The usual "splat" sound had not been heard. The vomit appeared to be suspended in mid-air.

"That's fucking impossible," a voice spoke.

There was no one else present in the room but Jacob himself. He was beginning to believe all of this was some sort of a sick dream. *How could it possibly be real?* Jacob gave in to his burning desire and touched his face. He felt remarkably better. Not just mentally but physically. His nausea and dizziness had vanished. The vomit landed on the floor, making a disgusting splat, just like it should have in the first place.

"That's better. Give in to your urges. Give in to what we tell you. You feel so much better now."

There must have been a microphone present, amplifying the putrid voice that Jacob kept hearing. *Was it all in his head?*

"It's no microphone."

"Show yourself, you son of a bitch!"

Jacob, once again feeling sick, wanted to vomit more than anything. He gagged but there was nothing left in his stomach. He was much better off before he insulted the voice. Having a revelation, he decided to try something.

"I'm sorry."

Complying with the mysterious voice wasn't something Jacob wanted to do, yet he didn't have any intention of experiencing that sickness a third time. Sure enough, he felt better almost instantly.

"How did you do that?"

"We injected you with something."

"Maybe, but there's more to it than that. How can you read my mind?"

"The Council sees all. We hear all. We control all. You cannot fool our system. Would you like to cooperate with us now?"

Jacob gripped his blond hair with both hands as tightly as he possibly could. He was preparing for the worst. What he was about to do probably meant his death.

"No," said Jacob with as much firmness as he could muster under the current circumstances.

He thought of Marlana. *What would she do?* He really thought of Marlana. *Would she give in just to save herself?* A pain that shot through his entire body interrupted his thoughts. Jacob feared blacking out. This type of pain was like nothing he had ever felt before. The last thing he remembered as he began to fade away was the perplexing words dictated by the hidden speaker.

"You will give in eventually. Every man has his breaking point."

Jacob lay lifeless on the cold white floor. His face had landed in his own vomit. In his sleep he was dreaming. He was dreaming of darkness. A neverending darkness. He stood erect, all alone, decorated in a traditional pitch-black Council uniform, hood and all, hair in a braided ponytail, and he was still. Lifelessly still.

9

The Clique

The room was so damp that Manfred could actually taste mold. Its thin brown walls creaked with the wind. They were made from the same wood that was used to start fires. Manfred had been occupying the small hut for nearly three hours now. He was beginning to wonder why Colonel Abel was missing from his office. Manfred desperately wanted to talk with an old friend. He had gained no trust for his current officer over the past few months, Captain . . . Manfred could not even remember the man's name. His shady dialogue and strange mannerisms did not allow for many positive feelings. The silence of the hut was driving him mad.

"I shouldn't complain. When I chose to take the job, I vowed to defeat the Union. Whatever it takes," he said out loud in a whisper, attempting to break the mind-bending silence.

All Manfred could hear was the faint sound of the ocean beating up against the docks. It was too late for any cargo ships to be sailing. The Imperial Guard kept a close eye on activity of any sort, especially around the harbor. It didn't really make sense why the captain wished for Manfred, of all people, to sit here, and bust a weapons transaction. *So, one of the parties were Alliance members from the east, and the other were Imperialists that planned on making some quick cash by trading our weapons to the enemy.*

"Whatever. I should just get up and leave. I was hired to mess up the Union. That's my job. Not winning the war with the east."

Wanting to include the Council on his list of associations to loathe, Manfred paused his thoughts; they most likely planted a microphone somewhere around the docks so there was no point in saying it out loud just for emphasis.

They had access to virtually every Imperial and Union city. Cameras the size of an old world quarter were everywhere. One could not always see them, but they were there. Manfred yearned for the strong democracy the U.S. once stood for, that he had heard about from his elders. But that was before The Game. Before the Council. Even the fascist, yet capitalistic, Empire was more suitable than the totalitarian socialism the Council forced upon its people. They were all slaves of the system. If there was one thing that all the citizens could agree on, it was these statements. The Empire and Union almost ran their own separate mini-forms of government. That's why capitalism was allowed in most cities; however, the Council was always regulating this, thus never allowing the rich to become overly wealthy. By no means, did the poor ever see any of this money though. The Council used it all to set up more cameras *or something. What did they do with all the money they "borrowed" from the people?* The borrowing of this money is what made them somewhat socialistic.

His train of thought was abruptly interrupted by footsteps. They were approaching closer and closer by the second. Someone had placed a hand on the doorknob of the hut. *They are coming in!* Manfred, in a state of panic, clutched a stinger missile launcher that was intended for his mission (just in case), rather than his normal .22 pistol.

"Jesus Christ! You'll blow the whole damn harbor up with that thing!"

It was a familiar face. Manfred lowered his weapon and clinched his teeth together. He would have rather seen three Council members enter through that door than this man . . . and he was not alone. He had brought all of his friends with him.

"Oh, if it isn't Manny, the freak. Why are you such a loser? Captain Benedict literally had to send a whole fucking backup squad to protect you. And you're supposed to take pictures of the enemy not kill them—put that damn weapon away!"

His name was Dan. Dan was a common name that could be heard all over the Empire. There were quite a few Dans around, but only one Manfred. The others, standing around Dan as if he were some kind of a deity, all glared at the outsider. A sudden wave of laughter broke free. Below the belt comments were used, all aimed at hurting Manfred's already bruised feelings.

"Freak."

"Loser."

"Shi . . . no wait . . . freak!"

Manfred tried to think of a way to respond to the onslaught of insults. They were supposed to be on the same side. *How could they?* Manfred truly did not know why they would not accept him. No matter how hard he tried they never even allowed him to converse with them. Manfred secretly referred to them as "The Clique." With everything that had been going on lately he hadn't had the time or patience to deal with such irrationality.

"I think what we have here, is a failure to communicate."

It was the only thing Manfred could say. He understood that he was outnumbered, and a direct insult could mean additional trouble.

"Hey, freako. Marlana, the Union girl, will never like you," Dan simply had to remind him.

More laughter. More finger pointing at Manfred as if he were some kind of amusing attraction that one would pay a week's salary just to gawk at.

"Well, I hope . . . I hope I'm giving you all a good time. I am here for ridicule, right?"

Manfred thought harder. A disturbing image entered his mind. He envisioned Marlana clasping hands with Dan. All of The Clique was having a grand old time as always, excluding Manfred. Their sneers burned into his eyes like bright lights. He couldn't bear to look at them any longer. The only thing any different between his vision and what was actually happening was that Marlana wasn't present.

Perhaps Manfred was envious of The Clique's togetherness. *Whom did he have to put his faith into? A girl that hates him more than the war itself?*

"No! Bullshit. You people are disgusting. Why have you never accepted me, damn it!"

Manfred couldn't hold it back any longer. *If he had to work with them, why couldn't they at least include him?* He wasn't asking for friendship . . . just inclusion. He was sick of being an outcast for no apparent reason.

"Let's just leave this little bitch alone. He needs to calm down a bit before we make fun of him again. He might cry."

Dan was now at the level of *really* pissing him off. Hate generated a glare in Manfred's pupils. He clenched his fists together so hard blood began to slowly trickle from the palm of his left hand.

"I'm trying very hard to keep my composure."

The Clique ignored Manfred and walked out of the wooden hut without saying a word. They knew they had won this round. Manfred now understood why he was so angry. Not just at them, but at the world. He knew now, why his heart was filled with hate. It was a scary thing, but he had become a miserable human being because of people like them. They were the roots of his evil. Manfred sat in the corner, staring at his black shoes. A dark shadow hung over his face.

"They are going to blow the whole mission. Just because they don't want to be in the same room with me?"

The intercom system that all Imperial agents were required to wear began to buzz in his ear. Manfred almost didn't take the call, but then he tapped his headpiece, turning the machine on.

"Manfred. An Imperial Coast Guard vessel has destroyed the Alliance's illegal weapons."

That's all he needed to know. Manfred terminated the transmission and honestly did not care what his next mission was about. Filled with rage, he had made up his mind. One way or another, he was going to destroy all his enemies. Anyone in his way would be eliminated. Some might call him a bit of a villain, yet Manfred didn't want it any other way.

10

The Black Market

After a strenuous day of waiting idly, Marlana had developed the shivers. She thought she might be coming down with some kind of sickness from sleeping in such poor living conditions. God only knew what could be growing in these dungeons. It was damp with little sunlight and there was very little air circulation—a perfect breeding ground for disease. Every waking second she felt worse. Her mind was playing tricks on her. *How could I be sick already? Is it even possible?* She had only been in the prison for three days now.

Five hours transpired; Marlana and her cellmate were then summoned by two of the criminals that were holding them. Imagining the worst, Marlana prepared to flee, if possible. She knew that there would be no easy way out. No escape route all mapped out just for her. *Perhaps they may try to kill me if I run. Maybe death was the only true way to exit this scenario with dignity.* These barbarians were going to "test" the inventory as they had mentioned two days ago. This meant that they would rape her before selling her to a new master.

The two men were armed and looked as dangerous as anyone else except for the fact that they continuously made bad jokes back and forth. They were bringing Marlana to the underground fair with one or two intended stops along the way. Marlana had heard of this "fair" before. Criminals from all over the land traveled there in search of everything from mercenaries to prostitutes. There was no other organized event on the planet that could possibly be any worse for a young lady such as Marlana. Wretchedness and utter disorder were the trademark features of this hellish fair.

For some reason the women had reached the fairgrounds untouched by the men who held them prisoner. Even the blonde in the green robe, despite her pleas, was simply ignored. Marlana thought her eyes were deceiving her. There were rows upon rows of tents, with crooked merchants selling their inventory deep within the hollowed-out forest. She had never experienced such a disgusting array of scum in one place at the same time. Marlana struggled with her handcuffs, trying to loosen them, but to no avail. She was about to be sold to the highest bidder.

A man clad in a pure white business suit blocked the path of motion for the two women. He wore a white old-fashioned-style hat with a purple stripe around its base. Everything about him was neat; his hair was combed perfectly. His shoes reflected all visible light to the point where Marlana's own fear was heinously staring back at her. Marlana gazed at her reflection in the man's shoes. She was fairly attractive, or so she thought at least. Her long dark hair hid her bright blue eyes. She had no intention of allowing the man to do anything with her. He intensely observed Marlana, her cellmate, and then he came back to Marlana again.

"Mr. Robespierre! Would you like to buy one of these fine young ladies?" one of the barbarians had asked the man.

"Vicks . . . Wedge . . . nice to see you again, gentlemen. I may buy one. Possibly. How much is the girl with the lovely dark hair?" he inquired continuing to look Marlana up and down.

"5,000 Imperial dollars or 8,000 Union credits. The other woman is less money . . . " he was cut off.

"I wouldn't buy the other girl. Her face is badly beaten. It takes the quality out, no?"

Marlana took the blame for that one. Not that she really cared though.

"One minute. This woman . . . does she have a tattoo?"

"Nope. She's clean, dude," Vicks said with a schoolboy-like smile.

"I'm not stupid, you imbeciles! Look at that smile on your face!"

Marlana was coming to the conclusion that this man was some sort of a foreigner. No American would have thought twice about a tattoo. *He did talk a little funny . . .*

"But, Mr. Robespierre! How do you expect people to tell which girls are ours, man? We are trying to run a business here. We are advertised by word of mouth. There needs to be a system of identification!"

"No tattoos! I told you before. Now get out of my sight you worthless fools!" With those words he began to wander off.

One of the men turned to the other with an expression of defeat.

"No, don't worry. There's one party that'll take any virgin. They won't know if these girls are virgins or not!"

"You are so right. Good thinking, man. Let's go talk to those weird guys and see what kind of an offer we can get from them. Ha! Killer plan, man!"

"Ha, ha! That rhyme, like, so ruled! Hey, ladies, it's time to meet the Brotherhood of Sin. It sounds bad . . . but, well, it is. Enjoy your last few moments of fresh air while you still can. Oh . . . my fault, that came off as a little mean. Ah, who cares, we're criminals, aren't we? Hey, Vicks, you hear that? That was a good one."

"No. I don't get it."

"You dumbass. I said something mean, and then apologized. I then took it back, because we're criminals, man! We shouldn't care about people's feelings and stuff."

"I care, Wedge."

"You do?"

"Not really. Ha, ha. My joke was better!"

"That *was* pretty good, bro."

Marlana couldn't help it. She needed to know more.

"Shut up, you assholes. What the hell is the Brotherhood of Sin?" she inquired.

"We're not sure, but we've never seen any chick we sold to them return, dude. I heard they sacrifice people to a higher power."

He turned to his counterpart who nodded his head in agreement. Just when Marlana simply couldn't picture things becoming any worse.

"Sucks to be you!" Vicks laughed.

11

Otherworld

It was like nothing Jacob had ever seen before. The world was colorful. The world was at peace. The tension in the pit of his stomach slowly faded. He was free of worry and concern. Even his fear of death had vanished. Jacob's interpretation of the phenomenon was tainted by suspicion. He believed himself to be dreaming and/or drugged by the Council once again.

Mental awareness suddenly returned and Jacob woke up. He quickly opened his eyes and saw nothing but darkness. The light was nowhere to be found. His body was engulfed in what appeared to be his own blood. Not only did his tension make a comeback, but it also intensified. A young Imperial soldier carefully placed a gun to his forehead. Jacob had no inkling where this man came from; it was almost as if he appeared out of nothingness. A shot was fired and Jacob turned over in pain. Touching his head, there was a large wet spot where he had been struck. Jacob rested his chin on his chest as more and more blood oozed from the open wound. His body slowly became submerged in red. Drowning in his own blood, unable to breathe, Jacob once again found himself in an altered state of consciousness.

In this setting, there stood Marlana, with her arms extended, reaching out. Jacob wanted nothing more than to reciprocate, and to his surprise he was able to; for a few seconds anyway. This new world then faded away and he was brought back to an extremely familiar place. It was his bed as a child. He could even hear his parents speaking downstairs. What they were talking about he dared not to decipher. Jacob believed that these were all lies the Council was feeding him.

He closed his eyes, only to wake up over and over again in various places. Some were outdoors and some indoors. Some were next to Marlana and others were next to rotting bodies. Their eyes had all been removed and were overflowing with maggots. Then suddenly it was back to Marlana again, and then without warning Manfred, walking upside down, was there and he held what appeared to be a large blade of some sort. Again and again Jacob entered and reentered various worlds. What they were . . . he had no idea. He yearned to leave, and that's all he could think about. Whenever he would wind up next to a past lover, a friend, someone from the Union, Marlana, anything peaceful, something horrible quickly replaced it. *They* were trying to break him. Make him soft so they could manipulate his mind. *But how are they in my head? How are they creating these visions?*

There were too many questions he needed to know about his father, why that Council member had called him a "chosen one," and now he couldn't even decipher what was reality and what was false. Jacob, with all his might, wished for it to end. He wanted things to go back to the way they were. He was willing to do anything to stop this insanity. Every waking second the process of mental breakdown would speed up. The delusions grew more extreme. Jacob screamed bloody murder without end. There was no visible way out.

This went on for six continuous hours until Jacob was in a state of near mental breakdown.

12

Jezebel from Hell

"You know . . . my would-be wife wasn't such a bad girl. I believed for a while that she liked me, but then the more I thought about it, the more I realized that she was forced into it. I mean, she never chose to marry me. Nor did I choose her; so that almost made it okay. She was the daughter of some pretty politician in the Empire. I never got a chance to meet the son of a bitch. Arranged marriages aren't the best. But an assassin from the Union decided to whack an Imperial officer that just so happened to be at the small ceremony. He was the murderer of someone's fucking kid or something. The ceremony itself . . . " Manfred was interrupted by his acquaintance.

"I'm kinda hungry. Let's stop and get something to eat, hon," a woman with semi-short blonde hair glared over at Manfred and smiled impolitely.

She crossed her eyes, creating a foolish expression, all in the desire to force Manfred to crack a smile. Manfred appeared to be rather annoyed and took his eyes off the road to yell at the woman.

"You don't even care. You just sit there and chew your goddamn gum. Don't make faces at me. You were the one that asked about my dead wife anyway. Don't ask questions if you do not want the full explanation. I don't half-ass things. If you want to know something from my personal life then you can, at the very least, listen to my story with patience."

His eyes were now locked into hers, expressing a deep rage.

"Manny, c'mon. It's me, your buddy. So what happened? Finish the story. Now I want to know."

She gave Manfred the sad puppy dog face, followed by laughter.

"She got shot by the fucking sniper and died. I didn't love her anyway; I didn't even know her."

Manfred believed he was beginning to come off as a little too insensitive. After all, he never desired for his wife to be murdered, whether he loved her or not. He'd try to be a little more easygoing from this point on.

"So shut the hell up you dumb little bitch!"

That didn't work.

"Not to change the subject, but we should be at the under-the-ground fair, or whatever it's called, soon and I want something to eat," she said tugging at Manfred's sleeve. He was royally pissed off.

"No! We're in the middle of nowhere, there are no means of getting food, so be quiet. Stop touching me, I'm trying to drive. Stop touching me!"

It was too late.

Manfred just didn't see him standing in the middle of the road. The impact sent the woman's head into the dashboard. She appeared to be out cold. Manfred had banged his nose against the steering wheel but wasn't in too much pain.

"Finally, she shut up."

Manfred opened the door of his car and quickly gazed at the front end. There were two relatively large dents in the hood.

"Damn, I doubt I could fix that, and it's not like you can just buy one of these things anymore. They stopped making these twenty years ago. Now, I'm going to have to drive an Imperial standard piece of *sh . . . it*, I hit some guy, didn't I?"

Manfred then realized that there was a man laying unconscious a few yards away from his car. He panicked. He prayed that there were no Council spy cameras out here on this highway, or he'd be dead real soon. They'd send out a scout to find the perpetrator within minutes.

Murmurs from the fallen body filled his eardrums. *He was alive?* Manfred took a few steps further and cautiously observed his face. The man was in his thirties, rather large, and wore the Union symbol on his belt. *Well, now that made it all okay.* The Council couldn't kill him for nailing a member of the opposing faction. Manfred helped the man to his feet and was planning on moving him out of the road so he could drive off without his tires being misaligned from running this guy over. Manfred was aware, from experience, that driving over humans could be bad for your tires.

"Hmm . . . he looks vaguely familiar. An officer maybe?"

Without warning, a gunshot echoed throughout the valley and a bullet entered the midsection of the Unionite. Startled, Manfred dropped the body, and it rolled off the road and into the gutter. Manfred jumped back toward his car to get the hell out of the line of fire. His first thought was *yet another fun experience with rogues,* but he quickly realized he was completely wrong.

"I can't believe it." Manfred said, as he realized the shooter was his blonde passenger, "You just shot him! How the hell did you know he wasn't one of ours?" Manfred jumped up and down in disbelief.

"Oh, you know, silly. Just covering things up. I work for the Empire—and I kill people. I have no job classification. They call me in when they need some dirty work done. That's what I do!" she proudly exclaimed.

"Jesus, you should NOT be allowed to carry a gun!"

"Oh, just get in the car. We need to get to that fair before all the good mercenaries are already bought. And maybe you can buy a new wife or something. Something fun. Fun like you."

Pulling himself halfway into the car, Manfred froze with one foot in the door and one still on the paved highway. He glared at the crazed look on the woman's face.

"You're real sick, Echidna. But that's what I like about you."

"Specify."

"How so? I said you were sick."

"Sick in what way?"

"No, seriously. I know where this conversation is going and I'm not falling for it again."

"Alrighty," she agreed, but started to pull on his sleeve again.

"You touching me is what caused that damn accident in the first place. What do you want now?"

"I'm hungry."

"I have no food."

"We have to get something."

"This highway is a dangerous place, it runs through the ghettos. We're not stopping again."

"I love you."

"No you don't. Don't even try and have that conversation again!"

There was a brief silence.

"I guess you're right. I'm a lot like Marlana, you know? We're about the same height and stuff. Maybe she's a smidgen taller. My hair is blonde though. Can you handle that?"

"I said we're not having this conversation again. You're a lunatic."

"Agent Vega?"

"What?"

"Echidna still loves you."

He reached over and patted her on the head. Echidna enjoyed it as though she was some kind of animal being shown affection from its master. Manfred was a little taken aback from her reaction, but figured at least the caressing impeded the constant annoyance of her speech. He placed both hands on the wheel and began to accelerate the vehicle.

"What the hell? Continue!" she demanded.

"Wait . . . you want more of . . . that?"

"Con-tin-ue."

"No," he said firmly.

"Do it now, or the next time there's a hit on you, I'll take it myself."

"You wouldn't dare whack your friend."

"I'm hungry! Do you hear me?" she repeated.

Manfred realized that there was only one way to console her. Only one way to make her endless whining cease. He reapplied his right hand to her head and began to play with her hair. If she were a cat, she'd literally be purring.

"You're such a child."

And they headed in the direction of the fair.

13

Marlana's Sacrifice

The world was nothing but a blur. Her vision had been impaired by some sort of weed that engulfed her body. It ran its sweet smell directly into her nostrils until she gasped for air. After a few minutes of intoxication, Marlana became used to the alluring scent and began to relax. The smoke embraced her mind with tender ease. She forgot about all her troubles and sorrows as she slowly closed her eyes. Her newfound friend would not be able to rescue her from what awaited, however. It just gave her a little time to relax before the big sacrifice.

As more herbal smoke impaired her senses it was as if the entire world revolved around her. Thirty men and women gently swayed their bodies back and forth. Their arms extended to the heavens. Cries, screams, and chants were heard from all directions. Marlana couldn't make out what they were trying to say, but she knew it was a form of communication. She was being honored by these people. They were her minions. A robust man in his early fifties sang a hymn from a book. The book was old and dilapidated. He wore a red suit, whereas all the others were barely clothed at all. Marlana wanted nothing more than to extend her divinity and give them all what they desired. The problem was that she herself did not understand their true intentions. Marlana knew, however, that she was their new queen. They had already murdered the other candidate—and that's why she was so positive they had chosen her. The woman in the green shroud—her former cellmate—had been strapped down to a cross and was engulfed in flames by sinister torches. As she burned up, the fat man appeared to be morbidly fascinated.

At first Marlana thought of nothing else but escaping before she was next. She then had second thoughts when they tied her upside down to an inverted cross and extended her from the ceiling. This was the Brotherhood of Sin. What divine entity they worshipped before the arrival of her, she did not know. Marlana only believed that in a mere few hours she had evolved to the status of an all-powerful goddess. They had sacrificed that other woman for her and her well-being. Marlana turned her head to view the hot glimmering ash as it lit up the dim and gloomy room. A weak light cast a shadow across Marlana's face. She smiled and tried to speak, but nothing was able to exit her lips. One of the men reciting the chant drew back forcefully.

Four men trudged down from an altar Marlana did not notice before. Throughout the crowd, which parted freely as the men walked by, they started to light torches that were randomly scattered across the room. This new light revealed messages that had been written in a foreign language. Symbols were inscribed all over the walls. Their wretchedness was awe-inspiring and their meaning puzzling. Marlana's vision slowly began to return along with the rest of her senses, which had been warped by the scent of the sweet-smelling herbs. For the first time since her arrival at the complex she encountered fear. Sweat dripped off of her face like rain flowing down a gutter. It felt like all the blood in her body had made its way to her head, sending a pulsating pressure to the top of her skull. She was beginning to have second thoughts about her divinity. Sheets of ancient fabric covered the back wall, behind an altar of sorts. Marlana squinted her eyes to learn that those "sheets" were really blankets of raw flesh branded with the same foreign language that was messily written all over the concrete.

"I present to you . . . the Higher Power . . ." The fat man announced.

The room fell silent. Purple light from an unknown source

entered the darkness and added color to the marble altar. A man or woman appeared without any explanation. With the occultists blocking her vision, it was hard to see where they had come from. Shrouded in brown robes they remained frozen. Although impossible to tell for sure, Marlana could only imagine that they were staring directly at her. She wasn't the one being worshipped. *It was . . . whatever was under that shroud.* Marlana gazed down and to her dismay there were bundles of wood piled up under the cross. The tips of her hair tenderly brushed against the dry oak. The four men that were sent down by the Higher Power were here to begin the ceremony. *She was next in line to be sacrificed to that thing in the robe!*

She struggled with the ropes and screamed. She bit her bottom lip until blood trickled down her chin, releasing itself from its circulatory duties. One single ounce of warm virgin blood smashed up against the deathly cold floor. The purple light was now distributed all throughout the chamber. Glancing up, Marlana gasped at the crude inscription of a pentagram carved into the ceiling. *This was the end of her world.*

"It's time. Let the sacrifice begin!"

14

Strange Occurrences

"I have nothing to say to you right now," Manfred mumbled to his partner in crime.

"I have nothing to say to you either. You came here to find out information about that Marlana bitch, didn't you, hon? We're supposed to hire cool mercenaries and bring them back to base in our cruiser. You know the one with the big human- sized dent in it?"

Echidna wasn't pleased. Although she did fit in at the fair, she still felt out of place in another way.

"They're not going to touch you with me right here. And no, I'm not looking for Marlana. If I do, however, see the bastards that kidnapped her, I'm going to cut their balls off."

"Just forget about that Union scum. Whatever happened to her, she deserved it. If I ever get my hands on her I'd kill her just as easy as I'd kill anyone else."

"Yeah. I would too."

Manfred didn't know what else to say. He was torn between two emotions. As much as he loved Marlana, he despised the Union. If Marlana ever interfered with any of his missions he might have to do something he would regret; and Manfred never regretted anything he had ever done, no matter how vile or treacherous. He understood that he was raised by a generation of citizens led to believe The Game was more important than personal feelings. A generation that vowed, above all, to annihilate the Union. Although Manfred's love for Marlana was twisted and sickly, he ultimately could not decide whether or not he could kill her if need be. His feelings for her were irrational and barely made sense to him. He openly admitted that he had no chance with her whether Jacob existed or not; she was born his enemy. Perhaps his defiance for The Game was the fuel that ignited his eternal passion for a girl that would rather see him dead than breathing oxygen.

"So, anyway, Manny, we need to find some guys to hire. If we get some good people maybe we can get a promotion! I'd love to be a secret agent or something instead of just a . . . hey, what am I anyway?" the demented young woman wondered.

"You're Echidna. You kill people the Empire tells you to, and that's all you need to know."

"So I'm an assassin? Why not an agent, like you?"

"You're too . . . too . . . you are out of control, that's why. You 'bend' a lot of rules. So, your job is to do the things that other people don't even want to think about."

"I don't see what the big deal is surrounding me."

"You're the only associate of mine that's done time in a mental facility. Personally, I believe those things just make people like you worse."

"Great. Everyone thinks I'm a psycho. Oh, well. I guess I kind of . . . am. Why lie?"

"That's the spirit. Just embrace your insanity, and I'm sure it'll come in handy."

"I like you. You're fun. Most people are scared of me and don't really want to be affiliated, be friends, or cuddle."

"Don't worry. I know whose side you're on. Let's just say you're a girl after my own heart."

Echidna was finally content with her company.

"What the hell? Check out those two shitheads over there. They almost look like Vicks and Wedge. Same battered old body armor. Same style of putrid red helmets, and . . . damn, it is them!"

"Oh God, Manfred! We can't let those idiots see us. They'll try to sell us something useless!" Echidna spoke with an expression of worry.

"Relax, sweetheart, they won't try and kidnap you with me here, if that's what you're thinking. Just calm down. I know these asses, and if they try anything stupid I'll take great pleasure in ruining their lives. No, wait, they're your everyday common criminals, I'll just shoot them both."

A smile reappeared on Echidna's face. She was her usual self again. Completely irrational. She suddenly felt a great admiration for Manfred. She gazed at him for a minute, something she had never really done before. He was wearing a gray vest and under that vest there was a white-collared shirt. Over all his clothing he was clad in a mafia-esque black leather trench coat. The bottom half blew freely in the wind. His trousers were some sort of black dress pants, which she liked. In fact, she was beginning to like the way Manfred dressed altogether. Actually, she was just beginning to like Manfred. Then she glanced down at his shoes.

"Buckles?"

She was appalled that he was actually wearing shoes with buckles on them.

"How silly."

And with that thought she decided to continue and create more annoying obstacles for her business partner.

"Hey, guys! Over here!" Echidna called to Wedge and Vicks.

"No! Don't actually call them! Oh, crap, here they come."

Manfred wasn't in the mood to deal with such stupidity. He was never in the mood to deal with such stupidity. Manfred fished around in his coat pocket trying to find a stick of gum.

"Anything that would take attention off of the current situation would be great," he thought out loud. "Look what you've caused, you crazed little . . . "

"Manfred! And a hot chick! Dude! Look!" Wedge exclaimed ecstatically while grabbing the arm of his partner.

"Wedge! And another jackass! Dude! Go to Hell."

Manfred hated these guys. He just wanted to rough them up a bit. At least they were fun to harass.

"Hey, man! No need to get all PMS on us. We just wanted to know if ya wanted to buy something useless," stated Vicks.

"Did you just say useless?"

Manfred couldn't believe that these guys somehow survived the war. The theory of evolution had failed him again.

"No, I said useful. Yeah, I did. No, wait . . . yeah, I did. Just because we're neutral in this Empire/Union conflict doesn't mean we're dumb," Vicks responded.

"You're not dumb. You're fucking retarded. Not to mention common criminals at that."

Even Echidna had no respect for them.

"Hey bitch, you called us over here! Dude, what's up with that?" Wedge was now angered.

Manfred grabbed Wedge by the armor and pulled him closer. Both men stared each other down for a total of three seconds.

"Please don't kill me. You're pissed cause we ran out of women and you wanted one!" he said out of desperation.

"What woman? Goddamn it! You fuckers have connections with the rogues, don't you! The guys that kidnap and sell people!"

"Umm . . . yeah, maybe."

Manfred booted Wedge in a very sensitive region. He doubled over in pain and lay motionless on the dusty ground.

"Effective body armor. What a wuss. And if you want more, oh, there's more."

Echidna loved to see Manfred beat on others. Sadism was a fetish of hers.

"We . . . sold girls to the Brotherhood . . . of Sin . . . " Wedge mumbled, holding his privates.

"What? They're a bunch of sick freaks. They'd sacrifice the Empress herself if they could. We have to go. They might have Marlana!"

Manfred's urgency for the Union girl raised tensions between himself and Echidna once more.

"No. I'm not risking my life to save some Union bitch. And we don't have an Empress. I'm seventy-eight percent sure she was made up so we act united and all that good stuff. So, let's waste these two assholes, and hire some mercs!"

Echidna's eyes glazed over with anguish.

"Vicks. Wedge. You're coming with us. And we're going to kill two birds with one stone. You'll see, Echidna . . . "

Manfred's schemes hadn't failed him yet.

"But I don't want to go!" Vicks yelled to Manfred.

"Then death awaits you," Echidna remarked coldly.

She had decided she'd prefer to remain on Manfred's good side, if his good side even existed. There was no apparent rationale for her abrupt change of thought. Echidna had never been known for her stability.

"Then I guess we'll come too, Ma'am . . . " There was nothing else he could have said.

"Yeah, that's more like it, you bitches."

Manfred looked over at Echidna. She definitely had that "thing" he liked about women. She was around 5'4" with an average build for a woman, fairly cute, for someone so warped. The wind blew her semi-short blonde hair around in all directions rather provocatively, almost making Manfred forget about his Union girl. *Maybe she is just a little too crazy for me, though.* He couldn't make up his mind. First and foremost, he had to rescue Marlana. She'd probably despise him forever, but she'd always be his woman, if only in his head.

"Once that has been done, she'll have no choice but to join the Empire," thought Manfred out loud.

He smiled and helped Wedge off the ground and to his feet.

"Oh, and about the Empress. She does exist. I saw her once or twice."

Echidna just laughed as if Manfred spoke of a mythical deity.

15

Rebirth

"Is the subject ready for beta testing?"

"He has been ready for quite some time now. He has been successfully broken. It took quite a while, even using the nanta-machine. We were concerned that the process was not going to work. Last time we had a failed case it was over three years ago. It needs to remain that way. Extreme measures were taken and The Man was forced to peer into his unconscious. Leave it to our magnificent leader to crack any feeble mind. Our fearful prediction occurred, unfortunately. The element that kept him on the brink for quite some time was his attachment for Marlana Von."

"Shouldn't she be another casualty of The Game?"

"That idiot Manfred didn't kill her like we had planned. Perhaps we should have spoken to him instead of simply allowing him to locate her on his own. Agent Vega apparently will not murder her. He's a lawbreaker. Not harming a member of the opposing faction? How absurd."

"It doesn't matter now. Jacob will be one of us. Just like his father, he will be part of the greater good. We will just have to put him to good use. I can assure you that he will not be a failure like so many of the prototypes. The nanta-machine is semi-new technology. It has been known to make mistakes."

"Oh, of course. The mind-altering drug cocktails are not yet fully adequate. The circuitry of the machine itself is truly amazing. If there's an issue at all, it's with the chemicals."

"The delusions that man had while connected to the machine

were exquisite. His pathetically high emotions for Ms. Von kept him in the fight for control of his mind."

"He was a strong one, but no match for The Man's technique."

"And what about the lookalike we sent out?"

"The lookalike of Jacob? He has been called back, for now. His work ended when he posed as the original and allowed the rogues to sell Marlana. They offered her to our man, for a fee, but he refused as planned. According to visuals she ended up with the Brotherhood of Sin. She will die for sure, and as long as she is dead Jacob will never return to his old self. He will be Council through and through. And to think, not a soul outside the Council knows of our neurotechnology."

"Totally ingenious."

"Now, about this Manfred. He has the potential of becoming too powerful if we do not suppress him. The Empire cannot ever truly defeat the Union. Then they may unite against us. Besides, his obsession with Ms. Von cannot coexist with our well-laid plans. "

"I'll talk to a man I have on the inside. Consider Manfred dead."

"Using the new and improved Jacob?"

"No, I have other plans. Jacob is far too important to us now. Manfred may be able to end his existence if we are overzealous."

The two Council members never moved an external muscle during their conversation with the exception of their lips, of course. Jacob had been given a new role in life. He would now be one of thousands of elements that made up a machine bent on dominance. Manfred and company has become the Council's next target. Two forces obsessed with controlling the known universe will never co-exist.

One hooded man abruptly glanced into the other's cloak.

"I must go to Imperial City Boston. That's where our new mission lies."

16

Shell-shocked

"Okay, let me get this straight. I thought you were a tough customer, Manfred. I was under the impression that you wanted the Empire to crush all her enemies and that crap. Why the hell are we going to save this Union bitch again?"

Echidna was continuing to have second thoughts about entering the semi-underground cult of the Brotherhood. She was brainwashed by a system of propaganda that instructed her to hate the Union, not risk her life to rescue Manfred's dream woman.

Manfred ignored her and stared blindly into the orange rocks surrounding the complex. His dark coat flaps blew freely in the wind. He then turned to Echidna and noticed something for the first time. She was being rational. Due to the weather, her blonde hair interfered with her vision. Sand and dirt rose up from the ground and covered her white blouse, instantly staining it with soot.

"Do you fucking see that? A good blouse sandblasted over someone I don't even know anymore. Urgg! Manfred. Manfred! Damn it, Manny, I'm sick."

Echidna tried to finish her attempt at a response but found it impossible to continue. Her mind was telling her lips to move, yet they remained frozen. Manfred's pupils darkened with hate. Burning through Echidna's eyes all the way to her twisted soul; he remorselessly damaged her little ego. For the first time in her life, she was afraid of her very own friend. The expression that was so morbidly plastered on his face produced wave after wave of tension that made her feel unsafe.

"We are going in now. These freaks built their temple on the center of a bombshell. Take a look at those rocks, the way they are all pushed up. That's one goddamn crater. The shell itself has never exploded, which means it could go off at any time," Manfred explained, finally releasing Echidna from his hypnotic gaze.

"Why the hell would they build their cult on a friggin' bomb-shell?"

"Must be a religious thing or something. Who cares? They're a little over the edge."

"You're a little over the edge. We shouldn't even be here right now."

"Well, we *are* here. So just follow my orders."

"No way, dude! There's like, tons of explosive material in that temple!" Vicks exclaimed.

He was taking notice of something. The sand in this area—a direct result from bombings many years ago—was beginning to violently strike his armor.

"Umm . . . Manfred . . . what the hell?"

"I'm not sure what's causing this sandstorm but we better get the job done and get the hell out. The sand itself—it's poisonous to human flesh. Chemical weapons of some sort used way back in the day. That's why the Council allows the Brotherhood access to this place. It will eventually just kill them all, so why would they waste their time trying to exterminate them? So with that being said, I think we have little choice in remaining out here. Vicks, Wedge, Echidna . . . let's go."

"Well, I agree, Manfred. But what if the mercs we hired don't show up? Then no one will have our backs! We'll die for sure."

Echidna had chosen the mercenaries herself and did not want to disappoint their head officer, Captain Benedict. Although she had never met the man face to face he was usually in a foul mood via a computer monitor.

"So, Manfred? How do we get in?"

Wedge finally spoke after breaking free of the grim realization of the terror that came with this region.

"Poison sand is just too much."

"We're going through the front door."

"What front door? I don't see one, man."

"Neither do I."

"Oh God, are you serious? We get to blow something up? No way! Well, okay, I'm definitely going in that case!"

Echidna appeared to be back to normal. Completely insane.

"You weren't going in with us?" Manfred coldly remarked without even looking. He casually walked up to a random wall of the complex and began to knock. Reaching into his pants pocket, he revealed a detonator and a small compact bomb. "Now Echidna, what did I say about this place a few minutes ago?"

"You said it was an unexploded shell? Are you kidding me? You're . . . "

"Crazy?"

Manfred finished her sentence, smiled, and turned back around, faced the wall and activated the bomb.

"Alright, everyone, stand back about forty feet. Or two hundred. Either or; I'm not sure if this thing's a shell from before or after the War of the Old World, so I really don't know. Let's just call it right now . . . forty. Okay, run, and then I'll detonate this son of a bitch."

"But Manfred! You might kill Marla . . . or whatever her fucking name is!" Vicks exclaimed.

"Yeah, maybe. I'm doing this for my friend, Echidna. Now, sweetheart, you know I really don't care quite as much as you think. Marlana could very well be killed in this explosion. Feel any better?"

What bitter sarcasm. Just for spite there was more than a good chance he'd kill them all.

"Yeah. Actually I do feel better now. But what if this is one of those big bombs? You know, the BIG ones, from the Old War! We'd have to run back two hundred feet, right? Wait, I got an idea! Rock, paper, scissors!"

"Damn, Echidna. I swear that sometimes, I wonder . . . okay, fine. If I win, it's the big one. Ready. Set. Go! Shit!"

"Ha ha! Rock! You always do that stupid paper! I win. So, it's small I guess. Alrighty, you boneheads, let's move out forty feet."

"Why don't we move back like, two hundred feet anyway, man?"

"Are you trying to make me look non-professional?"

"No . . ."

They walked through the sand for about four minutes and waited for Manfred to detonate the bomb. Wedge turned to his counterpart, Vicks, and gave him a sudden hug. Echidna started laughing and mocking them but Manfred found it difficult to concentrate. He really had no idea how large that bomb was. The cult itself was far enough under the ground that the blast may or may not kill everyone inside. Either way Marlana would eventually die. It was time to take an almost foolish risk.

"Marlana . . . forgive me."

Manfred removed the trigger guard and detonated the bomb. Sand, sand, sand, and large hot shards of metal flew into the atmosphere. It was raining fire and brimstone. After all of the shrapnel had finally fallen back down to earth, Manfred rose to his feet and looked around for Echidna. She was half buried under the dark yellow sand. Manfred took a few seconds to laugh at her before helping her out.

"Funny. Really funny. That sand is poisonous! Do you realize what we're breathing in now?"

Echidna's face was blackened with soot. She desperately tried to cover her mouth from the fumes.

"That means we better hurry up and get inside, then. What a mess I just caused."

"Now we have to crawl through burning shit to enter?"

"Don't worry. You'll have fun when we reach the bottom. I'm

sure they'll be plenty of people left for you to . . . play with. God, you're sick. Where did you go wrong, woman?"

"Just shut up and let's get in there before we develop cancer."

Manfred glanced over his shoulder and did not see Vicks or Wedge. Wearing heavy armor really wasn't a good thing for a sandstorm.

"They brought us here at least. Oh well, they served their purpose. Let's go."

17

From Bad to Worse

Her eyelids were swollen shut by a deep hatred. The effects of the drug that freely floated in the stale, dry air had worn off and now Marlana was alone once more. The desire for Jacob's presence grew to a breaking point of no return. She just couldn't take it any longer. *Had Jacob passed on an opportunity to buy her back from those rogues?* Marlana honestly had no idea. She didn't even know if Jacob was still breathing. Tension had crept up behind her like the stealth of an assassin. All around her people screamed in pain. A sudden rupture had caused the ceiling to cave in, severely weakening the Brotherhood. Next to her, a man's fallen body slowly turned to charcoal.

"Define irony."

Marlana was barely able to speak. Her throat burned from the accumulation of sorrow. Although she loathed the sour smell of smoldering human flesh, there was nothing she could do trapped under a pile of rubble.

Marlana searched for the fat man but didn't see him. He had either already escaped or was crushed to death. She was hoping he was crushed to death. Someone was approaching her from behind but she was too worn out to care. They stood still . . . barely breathing. Her heart turned black and joined with the surrounding darkness. She experienced true hate for the first time in all her life. To her right, a member of the cult murmured something about a higher power and crawled on top of her body. The extra weight was killing her leg, which was probably broken somewhere under thirty pounds of rock. Marlana did not care what happened to her next. If she could only save the world and its peoples, she'd sacrifice herself. This was her way of doing so. Not that she had much of a choice.

"The least you can do is look. Guess who, sweetheart!"

It was the man that needed no introduction in Marlana's book of villains.

"Stupid Brotherhood of Sin, I'll show you who can sin. You want to worship the devil. You should be worshipping me."

Manfred blew a hole through the man's head. Once again, Marlana was covered in blood.

"What the hell are you doing here?"

It was no big surprise. He seemed to follow her wherever she ended up.

"I'm here to rescue you. Give me some credit. I could have let the heathens slaughter you, or burn you, or whatever they do."

"I'd rather die than leave this miserable place with you!"

"So, you'd take a miserable place that happens to be on fire, than a miserable man that would be completely extinguished if you were to come with him."

"What are you talking about?"

"You'd put out my fire, sort to speak. You know, my intense dislike for everyone."

"You're sick!"

"Oh, really?"

"Yeah."

"Manfred, look what I took off of a dead guy. And I killed that dead guy too. Hee, he-he!"

Echidna had found the pair in the midst of chaos.

"A sword. It appears to be a katana. Not bad. I could use a close range weapon like this."

Manfred read the inscription on the side of its hilt: *Kaiser's Revenge.*

"I like its name as well. Not sure what it means, but I'll find out someday, I guess."

Echidna handed over the blade to Manfred and gazed at the fallen Marlana. Her head burned with confusion. *Marlana Von? This is just too much. What have you become?* Marlana, noticing an uneasy tension, looked up at Echidna. *This is unbelievable.*

"Am I missing something? Why are you two staring at each other?" Manfred asked, pausing before lifting some rubble out of Marlana's way.

He bent down and attempted to pull her up. Echidna appeared to be sick to her stomach, and Marlana was literally shaking. She wasn't even shaking when she anticipated being burned alive.

"I am really going to enjoy this now, Marlana. You're lucky Manfred is here. You hate him, but he just saved your life. Not from the Brotherhood, but from me," Echidna bluntly stated. "BUT, he's going to take you away. A prisoner of the Empire. Now, there are no cameras here, so it's safe to say we're not big fans of the Council and their b.s., but you and your Union shall die first. We really don't care about you, little girl. That's what makes us the stronger ones."

An emotionless Echidna stepped back and kicked a fallen body in the head.

"Do as you will: the Empire is going to be destroyed internally by people like you."

Marlana's eyes glazed over with tears. She did all she could to hold them back. Her voice began to choke up on her.

"Just do as you will."

She brushed her long dark hair out of her face and waited for a response.

"I don't know what the hell is going on here, but Marlana, work with me. I'm trying to set you free of this rubble."

Manfred was shocked to see Echidna so distraught over this. *There must be more to it than a simple Union/Empire conflict.*

"Echidna, we'll talk some other time. Right now, help me get Marlana out of here."

Reluctantly, Echidna aided Manfred, but never unlocked her sinister gaze from Marlana.

"You know what, Manny? I've got the perfect revenge. Something that'll be good for the both of us. Something that'll get my mind off of the fact the mercs we hired never showed. Something to ease my pain of seeing her," she said and then smiled and turned to Manfred. "Force her to marry you."

"You know, I like the sound of that one. You're hurting her, and helping me at the same time. Perhaps you have come up with a fate worse than death for our friend? Now you shouldn't have the desire to kill her, baby. Now, that's the Echidna I know and love," Manfred laughed, almost taunting his Marlana.

"You. You are going to marry me."

Marlana's worst nightmare was on the verge of coming true. She couldn't even speak. She was too weak.

"Yes. The Union took a wife from me, so now they can give me another one," said Manfred as his eyes gleamed with delight.

"So, now all we need is a ring and we'll be golden, sweetheart! You know if phones weren't illegal nationwide or they still worked, I'd call up Council headquarters or whatever it's referred to and ask for Jacob. I'd tell him the good news. Oh, this is be-aut-iful!"

"I hope you're pleased with yourself."

"I am."

"I thought so. And that's sad. Really fucking sad."

"I waited a long time for this, Marlana. I dedicated a large portion of my life to you. Why I love you, I really don't know. It's as if I can't control it. Now I know that sometimes I'm a bit harsh, but I wouldn't be nearly so bad if I had you," Manfred said as his face lit up and he grew more sensitive.

"Jacob is more of a man than you will ever be."

"Jacob is not here," Echidna piped in.

"Be quiet. I need to have this conversation with her!" yelled Manfred.

"I don't care what you have to say. I'm not listening."

"Marlana . . . there's many Jacobs in this world. But only one of me. Granted he may seem like a good boyfriend, but he'd leave you if someone he thought was better came along. I don't think there is anyone any better. I will remain loyal to you forever. Why pass this up?"

"Because, Manfred, you are an evil son of a bitch."

"Too bad you don't see things my way. I really hope you enjoyed experiencing my sensitive side for those few seconds because you may never see it again. Years ago I attempted to win you over in a normal fashion, but since that wasn't going to happen, I have to resort to this."

"How were you supposed to win me over in a normal fashion? There are laws against us even being friends."

"Those laws cannot exist forever. You may not see it now, but someday you will be very grateful I decided to rescue you and take you in."

"Never."

"Our only problem, despite your heroic nonsense, is that we have a failure to communicate. Don't try and be a hero, please. I kill heroes for a living."

Echidna stood amongst the burning rubble, surrounded by flames. She began to make extended eye-contact with Marlana again, but this time her eyes were not filled with hate. She just had that look on her face. The one that said: *We just screwed you, big time.* Manfred took a step back and observed the situation. He had finally won. Marlana was saying something to Echidna but he didn't even pay attention. There was only one thing that mattered now. Soon, he would be complete.

18

Portland

"I am proud to announce that today is the dawning of a new beginning. Today, the Union is something more. We will continue to wage war against the corrupt Empire of Despair; however, we are now equally as powerful as our foe. No longer will this faction be known as the weaker of the two entities. Together, we shall overcome all obstacles and survive!" the spokesman for the group concluded his speech.

"Long live the Union!"

A massive cheer echoed throughout the entire complex. Somewhere between three and five thousand Union soldiers, supporters, and visionaries were present. The event itself was being held at the Union's largest and strongest compound, an abandoned factory of the Old World. Council operated cameras dangled from the ceiling like spiders. There must have been one for every ten citizens.

The structure of the Union was here, in a small secluded area of the known world called Portland. Rows and rows of Union troops lined the aisles as their supporters grew silent. The sun's glare entered the factory through a large hole in the ceiling and lit up the brown helmets of the soldiers, giving them all an aura of hope. Hope that someday they no longer had to be here anticipating battle. The crowd was silent.

One of the men closed his eyes to think. Sweat poured down the shaft of his rifle as the gun was suspended between his quivering hands. His green uniform, stained with dirt and blood, suddenly felt uncomfortable to wear. He never wanted his army fatigues to feel this way. His uniform would be the last thing he'd wear before he died. At least he was one of the lucky ones to even be issued fatigues. The Union did not have the resources to supply every soldier with the proper equipment.

This was the first time the Union had had enough means to manufacture any custom uniforms, even if they were made out of old faded material, and all he wanted to do was wear it without the fear of death. He stared down at the plain green and viewed all the bloodstains. Some were his; some weren't. He hoped he would never have to experience his own blood being smeared into his clothes again. *Then again, who would?*

"You look tense. Calm down, we'll be relieved of duty after he gives his speech," a man the soldier hardly knew informed him.

"Yeah. It's just that I can't bear to think there's a guy that wants the Empire and Union to be one. He's going to be arrested by Council police. And if they show up, we'll all go down with him."

After speaking his piece, he began to shake uncontrollably. That's all the soldier could think about was being executed as part of a conspiracy. It's times like this that he regretted becoming a soldier and not a merchant, manufacturer, or even a farmer. He had signed up to fight in the Union army because he did not want to give any of his hard-earned money back to the Council. If he were to take over the family business and sell baked goods in the marketplace of his hometown, then the Council would demand a chunk of his salary. At least being a soldier, he owed no one. The Council never bothered to harass soldiers for valuables because they were fighting the war that kept them in power. And by taking large sums of money from common citizens they were able to steal while keeping the less fortunate Unionites as poor as ever.

It was a bit different for the Empire because their form of government was not a democracy. Various citizens could remain rich if the government decided to take special care of them for obeying orders; granted the Council did not make any exceptions themselves and still scrounged whatever money they could from every citizen. Although both factions had their own version of government, the Council was the ominous overlord of the known earth, and change did not appear to be on the horizon.

"Hey, pay attention, man. Atkins is about to talk!" a civilian yelled.

An old man in his fifties slowly trudged up steel steps and onto the platform. He raised his hands for the crowd to cease their talking. He wore a green robe. The Union symbol was sown onto the right sleeve. Five guards surrounded him; one stood out. A man with brown hair coldly glared at the first row of Union supporters. The grim-faced bodyguard looked like a car had hit him. His nose was broken, bandages covered his midsection, and he walked with a terrible limp. The old man picked up the voice amplifier and began to speak.

"We, the Union, were once part of the Empire."

The factory was so silent one could hear a mouse run by.

"We left the Empire long ago, after a great war, because they did not see eye to eye with us politically. The Empire was still referred to as the U.S. back then, whereas we declared a new constitution and dubbed ourselves the Union. Perhaps it's our fault that The Game exists today. Perhaps we never should have established a separate nation from the other Americans. Before The Game, the unified country was more democratic. Why did we split, then? Over political disputes that should never have grown so ugly. Over decisions made by the unified government that, as hard as it was, should have been overlooked out of the fear of anarchy. The Council, coming to power, did not allow us to re-unite. And they took the situation to a new level of terror! Both factions were then never allowed to intermarry, or communicate unless it was furthering The Game. We all know why we are forced to fight! So, the Council can continue its tyrannical rule! We are nothing but puppets! All of us!"

Atkins paused his speech to hear the reaction of the crowd.

77

Dead silence. His grim-faced bodyguard stared in disbelief. No one else moved a muscle. There was no doubt in anyone's mind that the Council was already coming their way.

With all of the Council's cameras in the factory, there were still no sign of them. They should have arrived by now. Everyone silently waited and waited, but the Council did not show up. Slowly but surely, sections of the audience began to clap. Other Unionites could not fathom what they had just heard. The nervous soldier turned to the man next to him.

"Call off the war with the Empire . . . and fight . . . "

He couldn't finish his sentence. It was on the minds of everyone present, but they simply could not express it. Atkins quickly removed himself from the metal stage and signaled his bodyguards to follow him. If the Council wasn't here, after what Atkins had just said, that could only mean one thing: something far more complicated was on the horizon. Atkins began to climb into a battered old getaway car, but then froze. He spoke to his head bodyguard with an expression of puzzlement.

"What the hell could possibly be going on?"

19

Conspiracy

The Council had small remote bases set up all throughout the known world. They were similar to Old World military bunkers in appearance but completely different internally. Inside each one there were about three master control panels for the local network to pick up all forms of communication. Up to five hundred monitors of varying sizes, revealing the personal lives of thousands of citizens, were present. It simply did not seem possible that the Council could keep track of it all. Yet, they always managed to catch every "law" breaker.

"First time inside one of our systems?" a man with a dark smile asked his associate.

"I've never been this close to the Council before—it's an honor," he uneasily answered.

Any wrong moves and he knew what would become of him.

"Good. I'm glad you spoke truthfully to us. We see all; we know all. There's no point in lying. Now, we understand you are from the Empire of Despair? If that is the case, then you must have heard of a troublemaker by the name of Manfred Vega. He's a real hard case."

The Council member raised his head to reveal his face. This created tension for his associate. He had never been close enough to see under the hood of one of them before.

"I think I know who you're talking about. I'm not too fond of him," the man said.

"Excellent. Then you and your friends will kill him at his wedding. It has been decided. That is your purpose. Fail, and we shall arrest you," he stated bluntly, pulling his hood back.

The Council member was bald, had thick eyebrows, and a pale pink face.

"Oh God," the man remarked, not being able to hold back his disgust.

"Is there a problem? Most of us Council members look like this. It's called radiation poisoning. Deal with it, you miserable speck of dirt."

"I'm sorry. My apologies!"

The man forced himself to be truly sincere or it would have been his life.

"Good. You're my inside source now. So, if there are any further problems, go to Captain Benedict. He won't lie to you."

"Fine, well, consider Manfred dead. And I won't tell anyone about my trip here or what I saw, either."

The Council member just stared at him for a few painstaking seconds.

"Why would you ever even mention that?"

The man broke out in a cold sweat.

"No reason! I'm sorry! I swear I'll kill Manfred!" he exclaimed, saluted the Council member and climbed up the ladder that led to the escape hatch. As soon as he was out of sight, another Council employee stepped out from around the corner.

"It's fear that gives men wings . . . "

"Do you think that fool will get the job done?" the first member asked without even acknowledging his comrade.

"It was your idea in the first place. We are going to kill him either way, right?"

"Most likely."

"The Man should be proud of us then."

"Let's hope. We need more men; then we wouldn't have to rely on such idiots as that man I requested."

"We are spread thin, but I have a feeling that will not last forever. The Man mentioned something of the sort to me."

The first member simply turned around and began to monitor all the computer screens he possibly could, searching for "crimes."

"I better not have come to miserable Boston for nothing."

"Speaking of Boston, the Empress wants to make yet another law that we will have to overrule. A law that prohibits large families from having to pay an excess of tax to the Imperial government. If their government does not have the proper funds, they will not have enough money to spend on war supplies. A Council representative was assigned to go to Despair and meet with the Empress and discuss the issue; supposedly it went poorly."

"She accepted our decision, I presume?"

"She had no choice. Yet there is something about her I personally cannot stand. Her arrogance is sickening. She should know what laws she can and cannot make by now."

"Well, no matter. Just think that four of her more trusted men are now working for us."

20

Wedding Preparations

"Just sit back and relax, you silly little bitch."

Echidna smiled and patted Marlana on the top of her head. Dressed in a pink bridemaid's dress, she walked over to a small wooden closet in the corner of the room.

"Alrighty. Inside that dresser you shall find everything you need to be the most beautiful Union scum in all of New England. Now, do not try and escape or I will take great pleasure in killing you," Echidna said while opening the dresser drawers, exposing an extremely fancy wedding dress that appeared to have been forcefully thrown inside.

Marlana was amazed at how exquisite the material was. She had seen nothing that clean in twenty years. Her eyes moved up and down the dress until she noticed an imperfection: a dried-up reddish blotch. Marlana slowly lifted up the grown to view the discoloration. She froze. It was just what she thought it was: blood.

"What is this?"

Marlana couldn't think of anything else to say. A large circular bloodstain haunted her wedding dress. *How was one supposed to react to that?*

"Blood! What does it look like? Oh, I bet you want to know why it's there? A Union assassin whacked the old bride-to-be of my friend, Manfred. I'm kind of hoping we get to see it happen twice in just a few years. Imagine being killed by one of your own, Marlana? I can picture that happening to you," Echidna commented. "So much fun!"

Her eyes burned a hole through Marlana's head. Echidna had the face of a schoolyard bully; only more insane.

"Oh, I bet you're tickled pick, Echidna. You've destroyed my life. Congratulations. First of all, I won't marry Manfred. I'm not going to say, 'I do.'"

Marlana shook with rage.

"Well now. Hold on one sec," mumbled Echidna during the process of leaving the room. *The door was wide open?* Marlana wondered if she should make a run for it. Even if she did escape from this Imperial prison, she'd be stranded somewhere in the middle of Boston. She'd have a snowball's chance in hell of getting out alive.

Echidna returned with a model of a machine gun left over from the War of the Old World. Up near the magazine slot her name had been scratched into the metal. It reminded Marlana of something a small child would do to claim a valued toy. It was a remarkably horrid sight nonetheless. A bridesmaid with grinning teeth, holding a weapon of mass destruction.

"There's something just a little wrong with this picture."

"Yeah, well, it's just to show you that I will be on the other side of that wall, and if you do feel lucky, then please try me. I'd love to make you holy on your wedding day!"

Echidna's laugh echoed from room to room.

"God, you're sick. Where the hell are we?"

Marlana figured she could draw some information from Echidna; she had always been careless.

"Boston. Duh! Oh, what building are we in? An Imperial base—a big fancy one. It's well taken care of and smells nice inside too. I mean, why do you even need to know?" Echidna asked catching on to Marlana. "Just get dressed and in three hours we'll pick ya up. Oh, here, this will make you smell pretty."

She tossed Marlana a bottle of perfume.

"Thanks, Echidna. I knew you still cared."

Echidna turned around to look at Marlana one last time before she left.

"Trust me. I lost my allegiance to you long ago. Now, do what I said to before, or it will be a fatal mistake."

Her eyes, glowing with hate, transferred their sinister path of sight onto her gun.

"It's waiting for you. How much fun is this?"

"You won't get a chance to use that. I haven't lost faith in the Union."

"Whatev. I'd like to see those losers save you this time. Speaking of losers . . . how's Jacob?"

"How am I supposed to know, you bitch!"

"The correct answer was 'dead.' "

"How cute. You think you've won, but you're just stupid enough to not even consider the obvious."

"What are you talking about?" asked Echidna.

"You'll see me in that dress, and become the jealous little Jezebel that you are. You'll want to kill me. Can a psycho like you keep your cool? I don't think so."

"I'll do you if I feel like it."

"And ruin Manfred's wedding? Granted it'll be illegal, against the rules of The Game, but he'd cut your head off."

"My very own friend would not hurt me. He thinks I'm a nice girl; he told me once."

"He has kidnapped me twice in one week. Yeah, he sounds like the type of guy that would spare your pathetic life. As much as I hate him, Manfred has dedicated his entire life to me. He will not let you throw his . . . hard-earned efforts away."

"If you haven't noticed, I'm pretty fucking unstable. Ask hard enough and you'll find yourself on the other end of a gun, or a knife, or one of my other friends."

"Fuck you. If I die, you die."

"Yeah, okay. Maybe the Council will kill us all for breaking the law, but you know . . . I think my lover man, Manfred, has come up with a way to marry you and promote The Game at the same time. Think about it. People will come looking for you. They attack us, and we fight. Manfred is smart—he said he'd explain that to the Council rep, if one even shows up. Maybe the Council will approve of this after all. So, don't count on *shit* to save you, bitch!"

Echidna left the room and locked Marlana in from the outside. Marlana, not sure how to react to all of this, rested on the ground for a few minutes and thought about Jacob.

"If only he were here . . . if only he were here with me. Things would change . . . "

21

Goons at Work

"Well, I'll be damned! Looks like the whole friggin' complex blew up!" a man with a red beard exclaimed.

He scratched the back of his bald head.

"Hey, chico. Look at these bomb fragments. They must have detonated this thing. Yo, I'm telling you, they must have made a whole lot of dynamite."

The Latino gazed in the direction of his boss to see what his general reaction was.

"No. There was a bomb here to begin with. The cultists must have been living on it. How incredibly odd! It's too bad we did not reach this wasteland earlier. Or, I am speaking for you two. Not I."

Mr. Robespierre signaled for his two henchmen to unfold a chair so he could sit down in comfort.

"I heard that this air can be poisonous. We should hurry along, gentleman."

His clean white clothes were slowly turning a shade of brown.

"Oh God, this is horrid!"

"I'm sorry, boss! It won't happen again. It's our fault, really. We were supposed to assist the Imperials and receive paper money for our services, like we have many times before. We got a tad detained. A man in the road needed . . . " the bearded man was cut off.

"Hey, shut up. The boss doesn't wanna hear all that crap."

He unscrewed the lid to a canteen full of water and handed it to Robespierre. "What's important now is we try and find a clue, yo. We need to know where those Imps are. Since we didn't show up on time, our reputation will be shit!"

"That's correct, gentleman. And since you are under my contract, I am partially responsible for your actions. I do not want any Imperials looking for me in my sleep."

The wind was severely tainting the perfection of his neatly combed hair.

"Oh God, we need to leave soon!"

"Yes, sir! We'll find something that'll help us determine their location!"

The bearded man reached into a small leather pouch that was attached to his belt.

"Hey! No chewing tobacco on the job!"

As the Latino warned his co-worker, he noticed two red objects moving toward him. *They appeared to be men wearing dark red body armor of some sort. And they had rifles.* It was enough fuel for a fire.

"DROP IT, NOW!"

Vicks raised his hands as high as he possibly could. The sound of his gun hitting the hot sand deeply bothered him.

"I'm defenseless man! We are going to die, dude!" he exclaimed.

"Naw, dude! We'll blame it on Manfred!" Wedge tried to rationalize with his counterpart.

"Shut up! Come closer. And walk slowly!" the mercenaries repeatedly instructed.

"Dudes! Don't kill us!" Vicks turned his head back, looking for his rifle.

Like a raging ocean the sand had already swallowed it up. Robespierre studied the two men and removed a small pistol of his own.

"What faction do you belong to?" he barked with a thick foreign accent.

"I don't know!" Wedge blurted out in fear.

"What affiliation do you have? Last chance to speak up!" Robespierre began to squeeze the trigger of his pistol. With his free hand he carefully wiped the beads of accumulating sweat off of his forehead, using his trusty handkerchief that had been passed down for generations. A purple "R" was sown into its corner by his great-grandmother in France of the Old World.

"What affiliation do you have, kind sir?" Vicks asked.

His teeth were clenched together so tight a grain of sand couldn't slip by.

"Just answer the question, gentlemen, or we'll have no choice . . . "

The man in white meant business.

"We have none, but we were kind of working for a guy named Manfred and his bitchy friend! They are Imperials! If you're Union, don't kill us. WE can convert!" a very pitiful Vicks whined.

"Boss, Manfred was one of the two that contracted us. Maybe these shits know where he is?" the Latino suggested.

"Good thinking, Chavo. Did the Imperials say where they were going?" Robespierre demanded to know.

The wind picked up and blew Robespierre's top hat from his head onto the scalding sand. Chavo hurried to retrieve it. He noticed the purple ribbon that was tied around Robespierre's priceless hat had become a tad crooked. Without much thought, the complication was rectified. His boss despised untidy apparel.

"Yeah. They mentioned something about Boston," Wedge said, looking down at the ground as if it was the last time that he'd ever see it.

"Good. Well, you two will come along and find them for us so we can apologize for not completing our duties!"

"But Boss, how will we enter Imperial City Boston? We don't have IDs and we certainly won't be recognized in the non-criminal world!" The mercenary spoke loudly, shoving the barrel of his semi-automatic into the face of Wedge.

"Easy, Mick. I am wealthy enough to have fake IDs made to

fool the measly border patrol. In fact, to help create war the Council doesn't even ask for picture IDs anymore. It's easy for anyone to sneak in these days," Robespierre explained. "Border patrol for the large cities can only do so much."

"Well, come on, homeboys, let's go."

Chavo pointed to a stolen Imperial marked car gesturing for Vicks and Wedge to get inside.

"I hope they're still not looking for that."

"Well, we can pay anyone off. Never forget that. Men, frisk these fools and let's get a move on. We do not want to miss this Manfred fellow. I'm sure he'll be happy to know that there are criminals that care about business relations."

A tear appeared in the corner of Mick's eye. Robespierre, never taking his eyes off of Vicks and Wedge, signaled for Chavo to place his white hat, decorated with a purple ribbon around its center, back on his head.

"Boss, you're the greatest."

22

He's Missing!

It was once in a blue moon that a Council member's expressionless face altered into a dramatic explosion of fear. His perfect plan could be interfered with now. From the Council core he received an urgent message that very well might alter history. Deep inside the Council control center he beckoned his comrade. This was their darkest hour to date.

"The Chosen One has escaped! A message from the core," the member said, doing everything that he could to hide his emotion when his counterpart had entered the room.

"What? The one they called Jacob has escaped? He was supposed to follow in his father's footsteps and become the next great number in the Council. What happened?" inquired the other member.

He began to cough violently at the thought of The Man finding out.

"He apparently passed all the tests, like we predicted. Only, he was given some freedom to wander around and to prepare himself for the tasks ahead. During this period, he just left the mother plant, and wandered off," the member said, trying to eat vacuumed food. "Attempting to find Marlana Von I can only imagine . . . "

"His future is as clouded as that space food you're eating. We have no idea where he will turn up or what he'll do. He may find out what has happened to him, and now that he knows some of our secrets, he will use them against us!"

It was the first time in years he was this excited.

Without warning, all the monitors in the Council control center faded to black. The lights dimmed and a soft but audible sound echoed in their ears.

"I'm afraid we've gone too far. The monitors and microphones are dead. We can't see the players anymore."

"You don't need to see anything, idiots," The Man coldly remarked over a small microphone that was once used to spy on citizens.

The member looked down and noticed the microphone wasn't even on. The power suddenly flickered, and then all the monitors turned on, revealing The Man's sullen face. As far as the Council member could tell, no live power was entering the complex at this point.

"Council Members twenty-seven and thirty-nine, I find your lack of faith pathetic. There you are sitting in your nice comfortable C.C.C. and worrying. You were taught by ME to never show human emotion. Now, what the hell are you doing? Showing emotion, no less!" The Man exclaimed.

There was something different about him; he wasn't nameless and faceless like the rest of the Council. His eyes were sunken and his hair was long, gray and straggly.

"But, Sir . . . if he did escape our plans may be altered . . . " the second member attempted to say when he started to clutch his chest and fell to the floor. He coughed wildly for a few seconds and then lay still. The other member mentally panicked, but tried not to show any physical signs of it, and was appalled that his comrade had died from pure fear—something he should not have even possessed.

"That was the weaker link. I'm hoping you are stronger than that fool," The Man spat out, making no further remarks on 39's demise.

"Yes, I am," he said, still not believing what he had just witnessed.

"You must realize something. Jacob was brainwashed and has

91

been programmed to kill Ms. Von. When he does, and I can only imagine he will, he shall be one of us. His feelings for her are the only thing that still limits him like the rest of the citizens. We do not make mistakes. We let him go. It was his time. I'm sure he won't interfere with whatever else it is you have planned."

The Man didn't wear his Council uniform very often. His robe was usually on, but was never decorated for such a low "number" as he. He forced all the other members under him to wear their pitch-black robes—and they all did. It was part of their training, it was part of them. Member 27 gazed at his master and motioned as if he was going to speak, yet stopped. He was simply amazed at how advanced The Man was.

"No, you don't have to do a thing. Just stay here and work the monitors."

"You can read my mind? How?" 27 asked, simply needing to know what made The Man so powerful.

He then faded from all the monitors and the power returned to the C.C.C.

"Things better work out for my sake. By the end of this week I want to see Jacob one of us. And if that foolish Imperial insider is successful, Manfred shall die as planned. Perhaps someday I will be taught all the secrets," he muttered, blankly losing himself in the computer monitors, seeking out "lawbreakers."

23

The Stage Is Set

A reverend waited impatiently for the bride and groom. He fidgeted with his black collar and found it unbearably tight. He gazed at the crowd that had arrived to witness holy matrimony. The reverend understood the situation and couldn't believe that a man he knew from birth, Manfred, had successfully kidnapped a Union girl and was now forcing her to marry him. Ten armed Imperial soldiers lined the altar just in case the prisoner attempted to escape. They were wearing the standard light gray Imperial uniforms; nothing fancy at all. This made the reverend a tad upset. *To think that people cared so little about marriage these days that they can't even dress up.* The common people that came to witness the impromptu wedding were just as restless as the reverend. They desperately wanted to witness matrimony. They didn't care if the marriage was out of love or not, they just wanted to see a marriage. A Union girl being forced to marry an Imperial gave them all pleasure as well, since the Union was nothing more than a scapegoat for all their personal problems. Quite frankly, it amused them.

"Good people of the Empire of Despair. I am Reverend O'Shea of the Imperial Church. I am here today to marry somebody and they don't even show!"

A loud chorus of boos echoed in the small Old World church.

"Where the hell is that deadbeat, Manfred? We want to see his Union bride!" a man in his forties exclaimed.

"Oh, he'll be here soon, my son. The girl he shall make that eternal vow with is Ms. Marlana Von; so this should be damn interesting."

The reverend, not even realizing that he had cussed, continued to ramble on.

"Now, this is the first time a Council rep has not come to a wedding in years! They are always around when there's going to be a marriage. I doubt anyone here bothered to inform them like we're required to. But they should know anyway with their cameras and such, and swing on by for the certification. But not this time. And they never eat any of the church's customary pie or cakes. Any particular reason?"

"Because they taste like shit!" a teenage girl screamed from several rows back.

"Hey, watch your fucking mouth, my daughter! Jesus, I can't stop swearing in public. That's what happens when I get nervous! The good Lord has cursed me for being so willing to marry that dastardly Manfred. Oh testify!" the revered preached. "We must praise God for He is the only thing the Council does not repress from your sad and lonely hearts. Can I get an Amen?"

"Amen, Father."

The two large antique doors at the end of the church burst open. Several people ducked behind their seats.

"Oh, it's just Sister Echidna!"

"Oh, it is, Reverend. Where the fuck is Manfred? No, don't answer that. I'm sure that silly Billy wants to look his best for this little bitch he's about to marry. Guards, bring her in!"

The sun from the outside illuminated Echidna's pretty pink dress like a jewel. She hung on to her machine gun rather tightly as Marlana was dragged into the church.

"That's it boys, bring her in here."

She lifted her head and made eye contact with Echidna. Marlana looked as if she had had a total makeover. Her hair was perfect, her face was touched up with expensive makeup, yet there was the morbidity of her wedding dress, and its large stain of red. The reverend squinted his eyes; his face wrinkled in shock.

"What you are doing is illegal and the Council will arrest and kill Manfred!"

Some Imperials left shortly after realizing that Marlana very well may have been speaking the truth. Others were here to witness a wedding and simply didn't care if they lived. They could care less if there was blood on Marlana's wedding gown or not. And the large firearm Echidna was waving around didn't bother them at all either. They've had become accustomed to mayhem such as this. Sad but true.

"No one gives a damn, Marlana. Life is barely worth living anymore. Duh! What? You should feel the same way, since Jacob got arrested and I'm sure he's DEAD! Besides, this illegal marriage, in my expert opinion, will only further The Game when your goons try to kill Manfred down the road sometime. So, will the Council have a real issue with it? Who cares!"

She made certain that she fully pronounced the word "dead." Echidna released a sinister laugh that made even the reverend cover his ears as though he heard the cry of the devil himself. Echidna removed a glob of gum from underneath her dress and began to chew rapidly.

"This gum tastes so stale. Why does the Council only allow Big League Chew? Urrg!"

"You are sick," the reverend said, once again accidentally speaking into his voice amplifier.

"I know. Sue me. You have a permit from the Council?"

Echidna looked insane. Marlana attempted to kick her but was restrained by the guards. For the first few minutes people were nervous about Marlana's advances, but then once again they became used to the threat of violence.

Both the Empire and Union were capitalistic and one could sue someone of the same faction in a court of that faction. Simple ventures such as that, or free trade and business, were allowed within each faction's mini-form of government, but it was the

Council that often nullified laws by telling citizens what to do and how to think by setting down an additional set of rules everyone must follow or die. They're totalitarian socialists, taking what they wanted from the citizens, their money and belongings, and then allowing them to go back to their daily lives of buying limited products, reading about the Old World in illegal books, and waging war against the opposite faction.

"Well now. We'll just have to wait for Manfred. He should be here soo-on!"

Echidna shoved the butt end of her firearm into Marlana's back.

"And when he does get here, like it or not, we're going to walk that aisle!"

Echidna yanked the head off of a flower in a nearby vase and stuck it in Marlana's hair. Marlana turned to Echidna with a look of inquiry on her face.

"What's the problem? I am the flower girl."

Once again the good reverend covered his ears to block out Echidna's wicked laugh.

The room was pitch black except for a small computer monitor. Captain Benedict appeared and began speaking about the wedding ceremony.

"And how did you know I was in the guest room getting ready?" Manfred asked, completely engulfed in darkness.

The only thing visible to Benedict was the glare from Manfred's eyes that was reflected from the monitor's brightness.

"I just shut off the lights, sir, and was about to leave."

Feeling a tad uneasy, he sat down.

"I took a lucky guess. There's something you should know, soldier. Our friend Colonel Abel has died of unknown causes."

Benedict stared at Manfred almost as if he could see him clearly in the darkness. Drawing suspicion, Manfred gazed into the Council-controlled camera set up on the wall adjacent to him.

"Damn it, he was a friend of mine," Manfred spoke rather softly.

He didn't believe Colonel Abel had died of "causes unknown." *There was more to it than that . . . Benedict simply did not look himself.*

"I'm sorry, soldier. I'm sorry, soldier," Benedict repeated, never changing his expression. His old pale skin suddenly filled up with pixels and then returned to normal.

"Sir, I think we should end this conversation. This is an important day for me. But when is Abel's funeral? I want to go to it."

Manfred quickly glanced around the room searching for an additional camera. *How did he know I was in here? All that is present in this room is a Council-operated camera.*

"I don't know. Know. Important no today you," Benedict was speaking nonsense.

Not like the Captain to talk gibberish, Manfred thought to himself.

"Am I relieved of duty right now, sir? Because there's really somewhere I need to go. We'll talk about Abel later on."

Half of Manfred's face had become visible due to a strange light that was coming from the monitor. Feeling threatened by the unknown, Manfred leaned forward and harshly glared into the computer screen.

He spoke coldly, "Nothing will interfere with what I am about to do."

"Yes, get ready for the wedding. Weddings. I cry at weddings," Benedict murmured mysteriously, and his face grew out of proportion and static filled the screen. Then the monitor simply turned off, causing Manfred to blink.

"What the . . . ? I have a bad feeling my luck's not going to change any . . . "

Manfred switched the light on and felt his tuxedo.

"No, we're going to go for the classic look."

Across the other side of the room, resting on a chair, was his lengthy black leather coat, a gray collared shirt, a pair of fancy black pants, his buckled shoes, and *Kaiser's Revenge.* He reached down in his boxers and removed his trusty .22 pistol.

"I was going to bring you no matter what. You'll come in handy later on I'm sure. I can't wait for the honeymoon already. Especially in Boston, one of the only cities still standing that isn't *completely* dirty and falling apart. Good times."

24

Unholy Matrimony

It was hard for Manfred to believe that a classic church still stood. After the War of The Old World, most vintage structures were destroyed or greatly weakened. As for the rest of Boston, like most modern cities, it had two very different styles of architecture; both styles mixed together. The first type of buildings were replicas of Old World complexes ranging from small concession stands to giant factories. Most Union cities were composed of these types of buildings. The second style was far more complicated. Modern dome-like edifices were erected, attempting to create a new standard of living; however, only the moderately wealthy could afford to live or work in such well-maintained buildings. Imperial Boston was a prime example of the present state of confusion in the modern world. Futuristic domes, gleaming with bright lights, built around crumbling war-torn skyscrapers. Life outside the heart of the city, however, was far worse—the suburbs were overflowing with ghetto warfare between the Union and Empire that never ceases.

A flamboyant, bright red banner was draped from a tall Old World building, bearing the Imperial logo, reminding the citizens of who they worked for. Manfred walked by and took a moment to marvel at the propaganda, before realizing that he was late for his own wedding, and hurrying on. Banners such as that could be found all over the city.

Deciding to take a shortcut may have been a bad idea. Just one block away from reaching the Church, duty called. Two suspicious convoys that slightly resembled Union buses for troop transportation were parked outside. They appeared to be waiting for something. Flabbergasted that no passerby found this to be odd, he decided to ignore it for now and jog up to the church before Marlana escaped. In his mind, there was nothing more important than his wedding.

"For the love of Buddha, it took you that long to get ready and you're not wearing a tux. Not saying you're not a classy dresser. I do like the black leather. It's hot," Echidna laughed, shoving the barrel of her machine gun into Marlana's back.

"Now, Manfred, get over here."

She turned to Marlana and whispered something into her ear that triggered a horrid expression. The once inspiring melody of an organ silenced the crowd.

Manfred approached Marlana's side and placed his arm around hers. He singled for Echidna to march behind the bride, forcing her to move. Halfway down the red carpet, Marlana attempted to flee, but ran straight into Echidna.

"Turn around and walk. Don't tempt me, bitch. Ha-ha! Dun-dun-dun-da . . . dun dun-dun-da . . . " hummed Echidna. "Here comes the bride, all dressed in white! Well, sort of . . . That was a lame joke for a wedding. Shut up, Echidna."

Manfred gazed back at Echidna after realizing she had just told herself to shut up. Her blonde hair concealed her eyes, but didn't quite hide her entire face—nothing in the world could have removed that twisted smile. She was enjoying this way too much.

They finally neared the altar. Reverend O'Shea gawked perversely at the madness presented before him. Manfred seemed delighted, despite the fact that his bride-to-be's beautiful wedding dress was tainted with a circle of red. Manfred fixed his dark hair, using a stained glass window as a mirror, appearing rather disturbed in an unhealthy way considering that Marlana was in great pain. Her eyes screamed for a way to escape this sentence of damnation but there was no way out. Echidna, clad in her pretty pink dress, continued to press her firearm into Marlana's back, making sure she couldn't escape. The reverend was torn between two emotions. He wanted to marry someone, but at the same time, one of the two people was completely against the whole idea. To help make up his mind, he viewed the spectators.

"Do it!" a little girl in the front demanded. "And hurry it up!"

"Well, if it's a wedding you people want, it's alright by me. Free cake and pie for everyone afterwards."

The reverend opened the Bible and began to read the proper ceremonial verses.

"I'll make sure this will be a fun marriage for the two of us, and not just me."

Manfred smiled at his bride. She gazed out a stained glass window, praying for some kind of a miracle. Time was running out.

"Come on, Reverend, cut to the chase! I've waited my whole life for this moment."

"Well, if you insist. Manfred Vega, do you take this fine young lady to be your unlawfully wedded wife?" the reverend inquired, already knowing the answer.

"I most certainly do," Manfred spoke quickly, mocking Marlana's situation, all the while basking in his own glory.

"Good. Marlana Von, do you take this man to be your unlawfully wedded husband?"

Everyone and everything grew silent. Manfred could hear his own heart beat. This was the part that they had all come to witness.

"NO! I hate you!"

"'No' means 'yes' in the Church of Manfred, sweetheart!" he exclaimed, tightening his grip around her arm.

Echidna cracked Marlana in the back of the head with her machine gun. For three seconds Marlana lay on the ground, until Manfred hoisted her back up again.

"Sorry, Marlana. Echidna's kind of a bitch. But she's really a good girl—she doesn't mean anything by it."

Instead of taking offense, Echidna gave a wide grin to her friend as if he was marrying *her*.

"Ah, whatever. I work for the people. They want to see a marriage; therefore, so does God. In the power invested in me, I now pronounce you man and . . . "

Without explanation the church began vibrating violently, throwing people left and right out of the aisles. The spectators piled out the front door.

"Just ignore it and finish, now! I don't care what it is!"

Manfred couldn't fathom that something would actually dare interrupt his ceremony. Marlana slipped from his grasp and dashed across to the other side of the room. She searched frantically for a way to escape her unholy wedding.

Echidna jogged over to the front door—it blew open, projecting fragments of wood into her body.

"What! Was that really fucking necessary?"

Manfred knew what was going on. Those suspicious vehicles he saw earlier were indeed Union transports. *Why didn't anyone notify the Imperial police? Or just blowing them up would have been acceptable.*

"Why does shit like this always have to happen to such a great guy?"

He frantically scanned the room for Marlana, but in all the confusion she was nowhere to be found.

"You fools. Kill the invaders!" Manfred ordered the surrounding Imperial guards.

Union soldiers stormed in and proceeded to take cover, while engaging in a shootout with the Imperials.

"Call for backup, now!" one of the guards yelled to another.

"I can't! All the transmitters are scrambled!"

Manfred, diving behind a confession booth, began to put two and two together. *Transmissions are down? Captain Benedict knew of my location a few hours ago even though I only detected a Council cam in the room. Someone's got to be doing this for a reason.* His head ached from frustration.

It was pretty much a standoff. Every three minutes another soldier would die, but at this rate the rest of this skirmish would take all day. Manfred had run out of bullets for his .22 a long time ago and just sat perfectly still under the confession booth.

"Out of bullets? Not as bad as me. I've got to take a piss so bad!" the reverend harshly whispered in Manfred's ear.

"Good way to get killed. Where did you come from?"

"I've been crawling around underneath the different booths. I can't believe this is happening to my church!"

"Well, that's the least of our worries. You see Marlana crawling around somewhere?"

"Not sure. It's so confusing in here right now. If we catch her on the way out, we can still marry the two of you."

"Good. Because that's all I fucking wanted. Now, if you'll excuse me, good reverend, I just have to ask. Got a light?"

"Yeah, want a cig?"

"Sure do."

"Me too, my son. I got some vodka in this flask here. The flask is old and made out of wood but it's all I can afford on a preacher's salary."

"*You* have liquor. Alright, I'll have a sip."

Three Union soldiers, without warning, dropped to the floor, allowing the Imperials to gain a few booths and advance.

"Look at that, Reverend. It's like that trench warfare I've heard about in World War One," Manfred said.

He started to take a long swig of alcohol.

"Don't talk of such things. The Council's new teachings claim that all history of the Old World was made up to fool the youth."

"Really? And they are teaching this to children in schools? Lovely."

"The schools have no choice but to comply!"

"I'm pretty damn sick of complying. I'm sure a lot of people are."

"There's nothing you or anyone can do . . . "

"Well, I don't know about you, Reverend, but there's a reason why I do the things I do. Out of desperation. I have nothing to lose, so I'm willing to take chances."

"Did you ever have something to lose?"

"I'm not sure. All I know is that I'm sick of the fact that every single day is the same. Every day is a carbon copy of the next. All our time is spent trying to resolve the same issue: to defeat the Union and win the war. It's not going to happen because the Council keeps this struggle going."

"They wish to remain in power. That's why they do it. But what can you do, Manfred?"

"I've just let go. Hey, I'm no hero. I can't help everyone, and I know this. But I can break a few rules and help myself. You know, I used to be a guy that played fair. But after all the shit I've been through with this damn war, you can't blame me for being such a bastard."

"Only God will judge you, my son. I see some good left in you."

"I . . . I have no idea. Maybe someday. But not now."

More Union soldiers dropped, and it was now apparent that someone was attacking them from behind.

"Now, what's this? One can't even have a fucking conversation anymore without something interrupting it."

Manfred looked around for a light. Reaching over, he grabbed a ceremonial candle and used it to ignite his cigarette.

Out of the corner of his eye he noticed that Marlana was making a run for it and exiting the church. Because of the unknown shooters, she was able to pass by the little bit of crossfire left. This wasn't going according to plan.

"NOOOOOOOOO!" screeched Manfred, standing up.

A Union soldier followed suit, ending his miserable life when his head exploded, spewing brains about the room. Manfred was now able to dash out of the church without being struck by a stray bullet. On his way out he gazed over to see what Imperial had fired that last shot. It was none other than Echidna, drenched in blood. A long thick streak poured off of her brow—she felt too light-headed to follow her comrade and collapsed on the cold hard floor.

"You're going to burn, Marlana," she mumbled.

Manfred thought to himself that he better find Marlana before Echidna did or there wouldn't be a thing left of her. For some unknown reason, Echidna's hatred for Marlana was so deep that she often couldn't even refer to her by her name. "Union bitch" was the only thing that she ever called her. At this stage in the game, Manfred knew he probably should just kill Marlana to simplify matters, but he wasn't going to do that. He couldn't.

When Manfred reached the outside he stopped dead in his tracks.

"Manfred! Dude!"

"Vicks? Wedge? What the hell?"

His own eyes were deceiving him, or so it seemed. It was like seeing two ghosts. Two really stupid ghosts.

"Yes, it is them. And I am Robespierre. These are my associates, Mick and Chavo," a man with a purple ribbon around his hat spoke.

"Right, and why are you here?"

"We came to pay our debt to you. We failed to show up when we loaned our services, yo," Chavo informed him.

"Services?"

"The underground fair. Remember, we're the mercenaries you hired," retorted Mick.

"Oh . . . right. Well . . . umm . . . go in THAT church and get rid of all those Union soldiers."

Manfred chuckled.

"This is too fucking much."

"Yo, Manfred I saw something kinda odd," Vicks said raising his voice.

"Just tell me, you idiot!"

"We saw a girl that we know. A girl we sold to the Brotherhood is alive . . . breathing, dude! New record," Wedge mumbled, suddenly having a bad feeling this was going to send Manfred into a rage.

"Where did she GO?"

Wedge was right; Manfred was steaming.

"Behind that statue of Jesus!"

He pointed to a large stone sculpture of the Son of God with his arms extended outward and his head gazing at the stars.

"Alright, fine. I'm going to find her. She can't get too far. She's in Imperial City Bos . . . "

Manfred flew backward until his body cracked up against the side of the church. Little bits of plaster flaked off as he crashed to the ground.

"Gre . . . nades . . . "

Union troops poured out from behind the statue, opening fire on Robespierre and his men. There were roughly twenty soldiers. The tip of a Union transport was visible behind the sculpture. Now he knew why Marlana ran in that direction. She was planning on making a quick exit with these soldiers.

"Well, none of you are going anywhere!"

The remainder of Imperial guards marched out of the church and began to give Robespierre and his men cover fire. Soldiers from both sides took cover and fired their rifles, handguns, grenade launchers, whatever they had, at the enemy; thus another fun standoff. This time, however, people were dropping at a steadier pace. Manfred noticed Atkins' head bodyguard, all the way from Portland, was leading the Union onslaught. Worsening every second, this was total anarchy.

"Karl, the fucking bodyguard! I thought that asshole looked familiar when I ran him over. Why am I recognizing him now? Shit, I should have finished him off. You're not taking Marlana! No one is!"

As the heat of the battle commenced, he stayed put for a few seconds, observing the chaos. With a dastardly smile Manfred rose to his feet and took cover behind a large boulder. He discovered a rifle, and waited to snipe a Union soldier. He then realized that a dark shadow had descended, blocking his vision. As he turned to see what the obstruction was, he wisely clutched the handle of *Kaiser's Revenge*, and what came next caused his heart to skip two full beats. His eyes grew wide with shock and his stomach curled with disgust.

"J . . . J . . . Jacob . . ."

25

Dead Man Walking

It was like a death grip. Their eyes were locked together so tight a diamond cutter couldn't break the trance. Manfred's jaw hung wide open. His hands tightly clasped *Kaiser's Revenge.* Jacob casually broke the silence.

"Sorry to bother you in your participation of The Game, but I am here to kill a Marlana Von."

"You're wearing a Council fatigue? Then you really must be here to kill her. Wow . . . being inside the Council must have been fun . . . getting to see all their secrets . . . "

Manfred wanted to run him through more than anything but was far too cautious for that. Jacob caught a glimpse of Marlana crouching behind a Union transport. He proceeded to walk through the crossfire without much thought.

"What the hell? This guy's been programmed to fear nothing. Oh well. Let them kill each other—my life's over."

He reached into his pocket and removed a pack of cigarettes. He dropped the box.

"No! No, no, no! This was supposed to be my day. Not theirs; mine!"

Manfred crawled along the dirt floor until he reached the church and gazed inside. Echidna's body was gone. In all the confusion, she could be anywhere. He turned around, facing the battle. It was utter mayhem. Union soldiers and Imperial guards were simply going all out on each other. *For some reason there seems to be an awfully large amount of Union troops in here, considering this is*

Boston. And no backup has arrived? Still?

"Well, well, well, I guess nothing really changes. A lot of people are going under now!" he exclaimed charging the battlefield.

Manfred rolled out of the line of fire and snatched an Imperial assault rifle from a fallen comrade. He opened fire for a good twenty seconds, dropping one Union soldier but running out of ammo.

"Crap. Nowhere to go. Going to get shot!"

Remembering he still had possession of a rifle that could be used for sniping, he took aim and dropped another soldier.

"I must be a professional killer or something. Look at that!"

Not long after his boasting was finished a bullet grazed the side of his leg.

"Christ on a crutch!" he fell to the ground only to rise up again. Running as fast as he could with an injury, he followed the routine of taking cover and firing, then moving on. He had officially entered the free-for-all.

Considering Marlana had been kidnapped roughly three times in the last week, she was in no mood for a fight. She remained crouched down behind the transport, still in her wedding dress, observing the skirmish. Without warning, a hand clamped over her mouth and pulled her upright. Out of the corner of her eye she realized a Council-issued machete was about to slice her stomach open. She kicked her attacker in a sensitive area from behind, then turned around and thrashed him in the throat. He gagged and stumbled backwards so his hood slid off, revealing his identity.

"Oh my God . . . "

Marlana's throat burned with the fire of a thousand nuclear warheads.

"Jacob . . . is that . . . "

He struck her across the face. She fell to the cold ground, remembering what the rogues had told her. They had mentioned that a man named Jacob had refused to buy her out of prison. She started to cry in utter disbelief. As tears rolled down her face, she watched Jacob raise his machete to the sky. One extended moment away from Marlana's death, he was slashed in the leg.

"Fuck this! Jacob! I thought you were dead!" Echidna screeched, attempting to stab him in the chest.

He kicked her in the midsection and threw her into the side of the transport.

"Jacob . . . I thought we were going to be married? I thought we were in love. I thought this was forever! Why the hell is this happening to me!"

Marlana closed her eyes, simply waiting to die. If what she was witnessing were indeed true then she had no desire to live.

"My mission from the Council is to kill a woman named Marlana Von. You are she. I'm sorry," he coldly retorted, preparing to execute the former love of his life.

Marlana abruptly opened her eyes. For a split second she felt something she hadn't in nearly a year. *Hope.* No Council member had ever used the word "sorry" before—it did not exist in their vocabulary. *There was still some human left in him.*

"No, Jacob, I love you! You are the best thing that ever happened to me! I love you!" she exclaimed, touching his face.

Marlana held her breath, preparing for impact, meaning for those to be her last words. Jacob suddenly froze. Confusion had entered his mind. He was torn between his mission and ancient feelings attempting to resurface. *Did he indeed love her?* Once again his train of thought was interrupted by the blonde bombshell. Pain echoed through his lower back.

"Try that on for size, motherfucker! Ha-ha! I don't know what the hell is going on, but it won't matter real soon, baby!"

Echidna kicked Jacob in his temple and roughly pushed him over.

"Now stay down, you fucker! Marlana, I'm going to make sure you die right here! I'm really going to enjoy this now."

Echidna licked her lips clean of blood from an earlier wound and stepped on top of Marlana's stomach. She strategically placed her machine gun against Marlana's throat.

"Bye-bye, sis."

"That's something you haven't called me in quite some time."

It was enough to detain Echidna. Marlana knew that after all, she was easily distracted. Echidna's normal expression of insanity turned to anger.

"You bitch! Daddy always liked you better than me. Daddy didn't care for Echidna, only you. Is that what you wanted to hear? Just had to remind me that you know my past! Marlana, I'll be seeing you in Hell!" Echidna yelled with neverending fury. "Ever since we were kids that's all I ever asked for Christmas was your death and Daddy never delivered."

"Where did you go wrong?"

"Ask our father. He made me."

"What are you talking about, Echidna? What did he do?"

"Ignored me. He locked me in the basement all alone. I was scared."

"That's because you, well, tried to kill him and collect retribution from the Empire, " Marlana mumbled. "Oh, I guess it wasn't entirely your fault."

Her eyes grew wide and she continued to cry. She was actually beginning to feel sorry for her sister.

"And he kept me in a teeny tiny basement for two years, alone. I only had my toys to play with. But you! You were outside, living it up."

"I'm sorry. Maybe our father had his own demons. He never should have hid the world from you."

Echidna stepped off of Marlana and lowered her gun.

"Thanks for seeing it my way. You're not so bad after all, huh?" she laughed. "But, sis, I have to tell you . . . I don't really care how you feel about me or my past. I'm going to kill you anyway."

She once again had her sights on Marlana.

"No, my jealous sister, Echidna Von is as dead as dead can be."

For the first time in days Marlana smiled.

111

"What?"

Jacob grabbed Echidna and rammed her face into the statue of Jesus Christ that had been serving as their cover. Painted in a crimson mask, Echidna lay still. Jacob tore the hood off of his Council uniform and embraced Marlana.

"I do love you! I'm so sorry!" Jacob shouted holding Marlana tightly.

"I knew it! I knew listening to me could break the spell! I knew you were still human!" Marlana shouted ecstatically.

Their joy was simply overwhelming. In the center of a bloody battle they had found each other and reunited in their true feelings. The only ounce of hope within ten square blocks was the happy couple overtaken with bliss. They had become one once more.

The clapping of hands grew louder and louder. It could be heard in between gunfire and explosions. The battle was winding down and the pilot of the Union transport was beginning to prepare for their escape back to Portland. The sarcastic clapping was still ruining the moment. Someone was certainly pleased with something. Or maybe not.

Manfred stood perfectly still with *Kaiser's Revenge* placed over his shoulder. His surroundings were ignited in flame. A black shadow ran from where he was standing all the way to Jacob and Marlana, concealing their faces with darkness. Like the fire, Manfred wanted nothing more than to suck the life out of everything present. He coldly stared down at the ground, then slowly raised his eyes to Jacob's. To Jacob it was like everything had been covered with a sheet of ice. Manfred's poison was leaking right into his love for Marlana. Now that Jacob had returned to normal, everything had returned to normal.

"We're right back to where we started from, boys and girls! This time though, I'm going to make sure you die in front of me. This is the last time you foil my plans."

26

Blood Feud

Manfred raised *Kaiser's Revenge* high above his head and charged toward Jacob and Marlana. Jacob deflected the attack with his standard issue Council machete and booted Manfred in the stomach. Manfred's brain was bubbling like a witch's brew. He could barely concentrate on the showdown. All he could think about was Marlana and how badly he wanted to just leave with her. Jacob struck Manfred on the side of his head with the handle of his machete. Steel clashed against steel. Manfred quickly scooted himself upright, powered out of Jacob's advancement and twirled in a circular motion attempting to slice Jacob in half.

"There's nothing you can do!"

Jacob knew that Manfred wasn't in the right state of mind for a fight. He was slow with his sword and out of bullets.

Manfred prayed that someday he could think clearly without his thoughts being clouded with Marlana and The Game. He wished to kill Jacob on more of a personal level and simply could not pull himself together.

"No! I'm so sick and tired of someone ruining my good time! If I can't win, no one will!"

Manfred rolled to the side of Jacob and threw a large stone, striking him in the arm. Manfred then kicked Jacob in the crotch knocking him off balance. Jacob let go of his sword; capitalizing on the situation he went straight for the kill.

"Marlana?" Manfred questioned, as she punched him across the face.

Temporarily blinded, he wanted to keep Jacob down for a few seconds so he could recover. Manfred heard movement out of his left ear and took a swing in its general direction. He had struck Marlana.

"No, I didn't mean to! Please! Get up!" exclaimed Manfred, regaining his control.

"Get the hell away from me!"

"Oh, come on! Give me a chance! I'll care for you more than he ever will! There's millions of guys like him!"

Manfred turned and attempted to point to Jacob with his katana but he instead experienced a warming sensation in the back of his head. Ignoring the strange feeling he continued talking.

"It doesn't matter where he is. Does it? I'm the one that'll worship you. Not . . . "

Manfred was cut off by a painful tackle from behind. He landed on his face. Blood trickled from his nose. He experienced the same sensation in the back of his head. He realized that when he was talking to Marlana, Jacob must have struck him awfully hard, splitting his head open. It hurt so much he didn't even feel it at first. Hearing Jacob's war cry, Manfred knew what was next. If he stayed still for another second, cold steel would have torn through his back. Mule-kicking Jacob in the stomach and giving himself some leverage, Manfred was able to once again rise to his feet. Half of his face was now covered in a crimson mask. Manfred licked the blood off of his top lip and glanced over at Marlana, gritting his teeth.

"I think I pissed him off."

Manfred charged at Jacob, kicked his sword directly out of his grip, and began punching him all over his body. Jacob's right eye was swollen shut and his hearing was impaired. Retaliating, Jacob grabbed Manfred's arm and rapidly pulled him into his shoulder, twice, knocking him to the ground. Jacob stomped on Manfred until he heard something break. Like nothing even happened, Manfred slashed Jacob's arm with his katana. It was time.

Time for this feud to end.

Winding up and preparing to drive *Kaiser's Revenge* through Jacob's heart, Marlana touched the back of Manfred's collar. He froze without making a further motion. Mesmerized by her touch, she slowly removed his katana from his grasp and tossed it aside. Manfred savored the moment like no other.

"I knew you'd come around. I thought you'd see things my way."

Two perfectly timed strikes to Manfred's jaw delivered him back down to earth. He dove to recover the katana, yet something told him that was a bad idea. Jacob's boot was crunching the bones in his hand as if it were a venomous spider. Receiving a low blow, Jacob felt a sudden rush of nausea from his groin all the way to his stomach. The urge to vomit couldn't have come at a worse time. Holding it in, Jacob retrieved his machete and blitzed Manfred. The two men exchanged attacks vigorously, their swords pounding against each other with a neverending fury to take away life. After several minutes, exhaustion set in and they slowed down dramatically.

Neither of the two could take much more abuse. It didn't matter how tough you were—the human anatomy simply could not endure such punishment. Blinded in one eye due to the thick layer of blood that was beginning to harden over his eye socket, Manfred knew he couldn't carry on forever. He decided to take a chance and threw his weapon as if it were a spear. It missed its target. Jacob couldn't have asked for an easier victory. Manfred just groaned and spit out some blood—there was a neverending supply of it. Feeling that he was drowning in his own bodily liquids he raised his hands, hoping Jacob would have some compassion and spare his life. Out of breath, Jacob ceased his attack and pondered whether or not he should kill Manfred.

Killing him would be wrong. It's not completely his fault he's so bad. He's had a miserable life. Jacob knew why he didn't cut it as a Council member—he still had the human quality of remorse. Even now he simply could not end the life of a helpless man. Manfred fell to his knees and stared at Jacob, attempting to predict his tragic fate.

"Jacob, he's only going to kill us later. Just get it over with. The Union army is about to retreat. We'll be left behind!" Marlana yelled to her boyfriend.

After all that Manfred had put her through she didn't want to take any chances that he'd come after her again.

A red smile of warm blood somehow managed to appear on his face. Without warning, he drew a hidden knife that was lodged deep within his shoe and jabbed it through Jacob's leg. Trying his best to suck up the pain, Jacob kicked Manfred in the side of the head. Jacob leaned over Manfred's fallen body and pointed his machete down at his midsection.

"I guess this is it. You got me covered right now, don't you? Oh, well. At least I bruised you up a little." Manfred barely spoke, choking on his own blood, finally accepting what was about to happen.

He felt a ray of darkness piercing his heart as he awaited his untimely death. He gazed up at the sky; his eyes were filled with confusion. Now and only now could he finally rest.

"Arrrrrrrrrrrrrggggg!" Jacob released a God-awful groan, realizing he had been shot.

The black in his uniform darkened with blood. Leaving Manfred, he quickly dashed over to Marlana, who helped him to the transport.

"A bit premature, but let's get the hell out of here!" Marlana screamed to the transport driver.

The driver removed a small voice amplifier from inside the machine and made an announcement.

"ALL UNION PERSONNEL—RETREAT! I REPEAT—ALL UNION PERSONNEL—RETREAT!"

The back door of the transport opened, allowing the troops to enter the giant vehicle. Jacob, being held upright by Marlana, was gently placed in the machine. They glanced over to see what was going on. The battle had apparently ended in a standoff. Imperial troops were gaining on the Unionites, but there was plenty of time for escape. Making a clean getaway out of Boston would be a task; however, for some reason, defenses seemed to be down today. After a few seconds the back doors had clamped shut and the transport began to roar away from the battle site and on to Portland. Jacob and Marlana were safe and sound for the first time in two weeks.

"Will you be okay until we get to Portland?" asked the officer in charge. It was Atkins' head bodyguard.

"Yeah." Jacob didn't know what else to say.

He'd just have to wait for medical help. He gazed at Marlana—she would ease his agony until he reached Portland.

"Jacob, I love you," Marlana whispered, holding him tight.

She was smiling; actually smiling. It was as if nothing bad had ever happened to her.

"I love you too," said Jacob.

He forgot about his gunshot wound. He forgot about life. As much as he needed painkillers, Marlana was his drug of choice. She was all he required for survival.

He had finally taken his life back.

Meanwhile, back on the battlefield . . .

Manfred was somewhat relieved that he didn't meet his maker, but at the same time he felt as though he no longer served a purpose. All his schemes had ultimately failed him, regardless of their depth. He blamed people like Jacob. People that always wanted to do the right thing even if it hurt them. Curious about who saved his life by injuring Jacob, he peered over his shoulder and what he saw literally made him gag.

"Hey, Manny. It's us. Your friends."

It was Dan. Dan and The Clique. There were four of them, standing there in the traditional Imperial grey.

"You look sore, man. What a fight! We were watching the whole time."

Manfred didn't say anything. He hated The Clique. Everyone that wasn't "in" pretty much hated them. No matter how hard he tried, Manfred could never obtain their respect. No one could— yet they begged and pleaded for it like a bunch of stray cats. *These people held too much prestige in the Empire for such a small and empty-headed group.*

"Nice black coat. Whatever," the female said. "We only wear traditional gray."

"Good for you. Thanks for saving me. I guess I owe you guys?" Manfred asked, looking to Dan.

"You don't owe us anything."

"Well, it looks like you guys finally came around to me. I could use a few friends."

"Manfred, we never agreed to that. You're even more foolish than Abel was."

"What? Abel's dead. Show a little . . . "

Manfred's speech froze. *They had killed him.*

"What the hell is going on?"

He must have discovered something.

"I'll tell you what's going on. And it's not your life! Hail to the Council," Dan mumbled under his breath as he fired two shots into Manfred's stomach.

He coughed up a little blood and lay face down, paralyzed with pain.

"Since you're going to die it won't hurt if I tell you this. I made a deal with the Council. This whole 'Game' thing was getting a little old and I was looking for a little excitement. Ever been in a Council control center? I have."

Dan smiled and turned to his associates.

"Okay, Dan, that's enough. We're lucky no one saw that! Our reputations would be ruined!" one of the members said worriedly.

"Alright, let's let this outcast die. We'll just pretend nothing happened. It was a stray bullet. Heck, I don't want *my* reputation being ruined because of this. No one can know our secret."

Manfred listened. That's all he could do was listen. It made sense now. They allowed the Union troops access to the city by lowering its defenses and scrambling all forms of communication. The Clique had enough influence in the Empire to pull it off without question. They purposely informed the Union of Manfred's whereabouts so there would be a confrontation to take back Marlana. And they could use the chaos of that confrontation as a cover-up to cleanly murder Manfred. The Council was the master puppeteer behind all of this. The only question was why? There was a rhyme without a reason.

Manfred remembered something. Captain Benedict. He knew of his location earlier. He must have been using a Council-operated camera to spy on him! Manfred understood that he was a bitter man and accepted it. Deep down, he knew he was a bad-guy. But he was not a traitor or a spy, and The Clique, Benedict, and the Council were far worse than anyone, on any scale.

But now that some light was shed on this situation, it hardly mattered as Manfred was going to die anyway.

27

Striving for a Better Life

Atkins stroked his white beard and turned to the peaceful couple. Marlana and Jacob stood side by side, arm in arm. The cold shadow of Manfred had vanished and it was replaced with hope. Although in Marlana's mind, she almost took pity on him. She didn't know why or even how, but she felt sorry. He died in a brutal manner by his own people no less. Jacob didn't care quite as much as she.

Marlana had finally rid herself of the bridal gown and Jacob of his Council fatigues. They were both proudly decorated in Union garb. As elegant as their previous uniforms may have been, and as old and faded as the green of their new uniforms, they were relieved that everything was back to normal. Portland was not as classy as Boston, but the friendly atmosphere was all they needed. Jacob understood that Portland was run-down and most of it had been rebuilt several times, thus making it a decrepit Old-World-style city. They were proud of their dwelling, nonetheless. It was a place to call home.

"So, my friends, it looks as though you finally made it back to our great Union city. I'd just like to let you both know that I've promoted you to commanders in the army," Atkins informed the two.

"Sir, that's great news!" Jacob exclaimed, overwhelmed with joy.

He and Marlana hugged each other as Atkins continued speaking. Marlana's head rested on his shoulder. Her long dark hair gently drifted in the calm wind.

"I'm afraid for your own safety no decorative patches will be able to be displayed on your uniforms. You are both wanted by Imperial forces and your rank must remain concealed."

"That's not a problem, sir, we're modest people," Marlana told the old man.

"Good. And now, on to my next point. Intelligence has informed me that there is a battle to take place between the Union and Empire and this time it won't be a small skirmish like you are used to."

"What kind of battle?" asked Jacob.

"The kind that may end us as a people. This fight will involve nearly three-quarters-of our men and women. If we lose, we'll be finished."

"We'll be calling the shots in this battle, right, Atkins?" Marlana inquired.

"You will help in a great way, I'm sure."

"Then leave it to us," Jacob stated heroically as he smiled at his fiancée.

"Boy, you have a lot to learn from me. There's more going on in the remainder of the known world than you think. I'll have to explain later. But before we depart I must say something, and don't worry, I know for a fact there's no cameras on this balcony. I truly believe that we are battling over a lost cause. Some like you, Jacob, and my bodyguard, Karl, who hasn't been in high spirits since some Imperial ran him over with a car, would probably never agree. It's just that . . . life would still be worth living if The Game ended and the two opposing factions, the Union and Empire, united to destroy the Council. I really miss the ways of the Old World."

Jacob and Marlana were completely taken back. Atkins had spoken of the mortal taboo.

"Let's just do what we're doing, for now," Jacob said, finally breaking the silence. "The Council, they have their rules. They expect us to continue The Game and never speak of the Old

121

World. N . . . never mind. I'm sorry."

"Those scumbags in the Council have almost made The Game a tradition that no one can even think to break. Even though the Empire is corrupt, there are worse enemies in this world. The Council, the great depressor, is one of them."

Atkins' words had become branded in the minds of the once happy couple. Now things were truly going back to normal: chaotic and full of angst.

"So, that's it. Just think about it. Think about it. Not for today, but for tomorrow. And your childrens' tomorrow."

Marlana wanted nothing more than The Game and the wars to end. She'd do anything to break the cycle of death and destruction; however, she still wasn't sure if Atkins was simply a dreamer. If she ever had the chance to end the war though, she knew she'd do it no matter what the cost. Jacob just tightened his grip on Marlana and treasured everything he had, fearing that someday it wouldn't be there for anyone.

28

The Seeds of Hate

Without any signs of life, the body lay face down over a blood-stained surgical table, draped with decrepit white linens. From the side view one could see the eye sockets were caked over with layer after layer of dried blood. The body hadn't been there for a long period of time—around a day or two. A short beaker half full of clouded crimson alcohol was busy killing whatever bacteria were left within its reach. Dirty bullets from an Imperial standard-issue handgun rested under the table. Red smeared handprints covered the floor all around the small room as if someone had been trying to crawl away after having extensive surgery. A brittle tablet, with a short verse etched into it by human fingernails, was gripped firmly in the hands of the faceless man.

The room's only door abruptly swung open and in came Mr. Robespierre, along with a surgeon whose appearance was as untidy as his surroundings. Robespierre's cleanliness stuck out like a sore thumb. This was not the place for expensive leather shoes.

"Surgeon. Is this man dead?" the criminal asked.

His eyes were fixed on the image of a heart drawn with human blood that had been roughly bedaubed on the shady cement wall. Its shape was slightly distorted due to the flaking concrete. Thin crimson lines of overspill ran to the floor.

"Yeah, he croaked a while ago. He was fighting all the way but he died. Good thing he went into shock before he finally let go. I ran out of painkillers days before your boys dragged this guy in here."

"I owed this man the services of our syndicate. Our valuable name will be crushed forever."

He noticed unsterilized surgical equipment drowning in a puddle of red.

"How horrid . . ."

"Hey, take it easy. There's something written over here on this tablet," the surgeon said as he turned the corpse over, removing the dead man's grip from the broken pieces of slate. The stench of formaldehyde ran through the air—Robespierre covered his mouth and nose with a handkerchief. A purple "R" was sewn into the corner.

"Well, then, read what the man wrote!"

"But . . . I could have sworn he died during surgery. Someone else must have written this and put it into his hands."

"Just read it, you fat idiot. I want to know what we can do to avenge this man."

"Oh, God. It's a poem of some sort. Take a look at this."

As I lay me down to sleep
I pray my soul is mine to keep
Never step outside this bed

Or unleash all the evil now back from the dead

"That's truly disturbing. Oh, well. Time to toss this body into the harbor and move on to my next patient."

Robespierre, upon hearing the surgeon's last words, took a few steps back and began to wipe the sweat off of his forehead. That body was not meant to be moved. As much as he wanted to warn the surgeon he simply couldn't speak—he was too caught up in the moment.

"Well, here, let me get rid of his guy, and . . ."

Manfred rose from the table without warning, and clutched the surgeon's green bloodied uniform. Like a man possessed he used the surgeon's body to help himself up and proceeded to toss the man aside as if he weighed no more than a child. Manfred pulled the blood clots off his eyes and licked his lips clean.

"Robespierre? Where is this?"

No response.

"I guess the dead do rise come judgment day. What do you think?"

Manfred extended his arms and motioned across the room.

"It feels so damn good to be alive, doesn't it? I can barely walk for instance, yet I feel so full of vigor."

No response. If Robespierre were a cat he would have lost a life.

"Looks like you can repay me after all. And I am not talking about the cheapest surgery money can buy," said Manfred, coldly.

He leaned up against the wall in pain. Holding his ribcage he slowly trudged over to Robespierre and looked the man in the eyes.

"I am alive for one purpose. It's a thing called revenge. My love will be for vengeance when I kill every single person that put me in this state. Why not?"

"Yes. Yes, anything you want. Right now you are hidden deep within the ghetto. You'll be safe here," Robespierre stuttered in fear.

"Excellent. The traitors to the Empire, the group known as The Clique, will be the first to go down. Them and their boss, Captain Benedict. They had it coming for a while. I think anyone would agree on that. Then it's on to bigger and brighter things."

"As you wish." Robespierre couldn't have said otherwise.

"After I take care of business here, we'll go to the Imperial capital, the great city of Despair. I have a feeling the Empress might care to listen to my plans for the Union. All their heroic nonsense! God, and that's all I wanted was love. Sure, I used some pretty underhanded means to try and find that love, but what kind of a choice did I have? This world is a mess."

The surgeon slowly lifted his head from the ground and gazed at Manfred in astonishment.

"Then, no one knows where I'll go from there. Oh, and the one thing to my advantage, the world believes I am dead. A dead man has a greater shot at life than anyone else. They will all find out the hard way that this cat's got claws."

Part Two

Unnatural Selection

29

The Clique Revisited

Dan carefully placed an arm around Suzie and smirked over his right shoulder. With his free hand he played with the decorative string that was attached to the hilt of *Kaiser's Revenge*. Its once brilliant red and black casing was smeared with grunge from the battlefield.

"Don't get smug with me," the Council member angrily retorted.

He walked over to a nearby computer monitor and stood still until it flickered on, revealing the harsh face of Benedict.

"I have gathered for you . . . for you . . . the following . . . a large battle may take place . . . soon, that very well could destroy one of two sides in The Game."

Benedict's voice was choppy and often interrupted by the annoyance of static.

"We were afraid of that. Well, now, that cannot happen, can it? The Game must continue."

The Council member switched off the monitor and pulled his hood back. Pausing to think, he turned to the others.

"Hey, man, I had something to say to our captain. You just shut the screen off without asking?"

"Simply because you are on your own soil does not mean that you should be so brazen as to speak to me like that. Do it again, and we'll find new pawns for the greater good."

"Alright, alright," Dan mumbled while glancing at his friends, Ryan and Dave, expecting some moral support.

He received none. His gray Imperial uniform became itchy and almost uncomfortable to wear. Realizing his mistake he decided to apologize.

"Sorry, I get a little emotional sometimes."

Suzie leaned close to Dan and whispered into his ear.

"They're such scary losers. Who do they think they are?"

"Shut up, Suzie."

"Pay attention. We have an issue. No side in The Game can ever conquer the other," explained the Council representative, completely ignoring Dan's apology. "Whichever side is losing will have to be aided by Council forces."

"You have an army?"

"We've been saving it for this occasion. If the factions want to attack one another with such magnitude then we shall deploy our own convoys."

"Holy crap."

"'Holy crap' indeed. Impressive is the best word to describe our army."

"What are we expecting to see here? Soldiers and stuff?" Ryan asked.

"You shall have to wait and find out. It'll be up to you people to make sure a few things work in our favor. If the Empire is winning drastically, then it'll be your job to purposely violate The Game, thus making it appear justified when we attack Imperial forces."

Suzie's face lit up with alarm and she opened her mouth to speak but, wisely, she decided to hold her tongue.

"If the Union is winning then it will *still* be up to you to make it appear as though a rule has been broken."

"How?"

"Lieutenant Andrews and McDaniel are about to be arrested. When we reach Council headquarters you two will be assigned to go undercover—behind Union lines."

Ryan took a few steps forward and patted Dave on the back. "We're ready to do whatever it is that you want, man."

"Good."

The Council member slowly moved in front of a camera mounted on a wall of the brightly lit room.

"They have agreed. Progression of plans is underway."

He turned around and removed handcuffs from under his robe.

"It's time for you two to come with me before anyone becomes suspicious of our agreement."

"Sure thing."

Dan gently pushed Suzie off of his lap; dropping *Kaiser's Revenge*, he saluted the Council rep.

"We won't let you down. You got the words of some pretty important people around here."

"Don't get too cocky. Now that is all you need to know for the time being. Be on standby. You cannot fail us. After we apparently lost a chosen one, failure can no longer be an option."

With that, Ryan and Dave freely allowed the Council rep to place the handcuffs around their wrists. Suzie repositioned herself back on Dan's lap.

"No idea what 'a chosen one' is, but we'll work out worlds better than whoever that loser was."

30

Empress of Despair

"Come closer, honey, I won't bite. Well, not too much."

An icy smirk half concealed by a black satin veil came to his sudden attention. Red lace was carefully sewn into the edges of the cloth, capturing magnificent elegance. Long blonde hair flowed from an opening within her headdress. With her one free eye, she gazed into nothingness, dreaming of her vast empire. Only fifty percent of the Empress' marvelous beauty and awe was allowed for anyone to witness. It was the law that she wrote. Removal of the veil had always been a capital offense.

"Afraid? Afraid of the mysteries that lie underneath this thin piece of material? It begs for you to push it out of the way, and then move in slowly, maybe even unwillingly, and kiss me. On the lips. All of them now, baby," the woman taunted.

A powerful maroon cape hung to her feet, generating an illusion of height. Her costume was carefully crafted by hand, and sewn with the utmost of skill. All the edges of the magnificent dress were draped with black satin lace. The base of the garment was made from the finest velvet in all her territory and dyed maroon, which just happened to be a color she rather enjoyed. The Empress motioned with her gloved hand for the man to come closer. Her mind was on work; she was losing interest and patience with the situation.

"I swear that I was not trying to see anything!"

"Oh, but you were, honey. You know the rules around here," she spoke with imposing authority.

Her smirk changed to anger.

"I have been waiting for a man to have the guts to lift up my veil and kiss me but no one ever has."

"But you made a law, Empress."

"I know what I did! It's for your own good. You wouldn't like what lies beneath."

"You are beautiful. Why not simply take that thing off of your lovely face?"

"Guards! Kill him."

"Wait!"

"Yes, wait. Guards, hold off. I'm going to play fair. Why do you think you're in trouble?"

"I don't know. You . . . two weeks ago you showed me a lot of attention. And told me that everything was okay. I swear that I didn't see your face, you just lifted the bottom, the bottom fifth of the veil to kiss me. You said that if I did a few things for you then you'd be with me!"

"Silly boy. I'm not impressed. Kill him."

"No. No! This is insane! That woman seduced me!"

Three Imperial guards wearing standard gray fatigues with additional plates of metal body armor covering their torsos, knees, and elbows raised their high-powered assault rifles to the unknown lawbreaker. A Council-operated camera, mounted on the far back wall, slowly changed its trajectory to witness the event.

"Don't worry about that camera, hon; I can do what I please in my own palace."

Shots echoed throughout the dimly lit narrow hallway. The only source of light was generated from giant torches that rowed the chasm. Two wiry blackbirds cawed after being startled and woken up from their nap. Droplets of blood splattered onto the red carpet leading up to her amply carved wooden throne. Spikes protruded outward from its base and curved to the night sky. The Empress tilted her head to the half moon.

"What a peaceful evening. Mina, I'm so happy we installed this skylight . . . Mina?"

Two non-military personnel entered to clean up the mess, along with the Empress' personal assistance, Mina Chan.

"Empress Gustav. Was there a problem today?" she asked, as torches cast a shadow across her face.

"No, Mina. Just take a mental note that I'd like a large framed photo for the wall behind my throne."

"What of the two bronze poles with the birdcages?"

"They can stay."

Red and black banners bearing the Imperial logo of a black-bird hung from the corners of the ceiling, decorating the gray walls. A small area around the throne was dedicated for the Empress' inner circle. Soldiers, advisors, and politicians buzzed around her grand chair, always trying to please their boss. Most of the time, however, the Empress enjoyed solitude. She wanted nothing more than to listen to the birds heckle and stare into the room's fiery light source, all the while envisioning a nation without the Union.

"You appear to be in deep thought. Can I get you something to eat or drink?"

"No, but I will need a glance into our future."

"Are you positive, my Empress?"

"Yes. The time has come to summon her."

"But . . . " Mina was cut off.

"Do as I say. It'll be easier on all of us."

"Yes. Right away."

"Guards! Mina. Accompany me to the other side of Despair."

"Empress . . . I'm not complaining, but do you think it is wise to come in contact with the priestess again so soon? And on such short notice?"

"Yes. Now, let's move out. I have business to attend to and then some redecorating around the office."

"Yes, Empress. Of course."

31

Two Jacobs

Marlana woke abruptly from her brief night's sleep. Biting her bottom lip, she felt the slow trickle of warm blood mix with the stale taste of morning saliva. Her eyes grew wide with the type of fear that nightmares are made of. She gripped the bed sheets, yanking them upward, then letting go. Marlana scrambled to her feet and dashed across to the opposite side of the room, knocking some books from a shelf.

"What the hell where you doing leaning over my bed?"

A Council issued machete slowly waved back and forth. The tip of the blade was the reddish-brown color of rust.

"You. Your knife . . . What the fuck are you doing? Stop!"

He just stood there. Smiling.

"I never got to really talk much with you."

"What do you mean?"

"Sorry, Marlana, but it's time to complete my mission. Stay still so I can kill you."

Thoughts poured from her brain to her mouth but she decided to say nothing. *He threatens me again . . .* She recalled her original tactic.

"I love you, Jacob! You're the best thing that ever happened to me!"

"Ain't going to work on me this time," he said while in motion. "I've got things figured out this time around."

As Jacob moved closer to Marlana she observed his hair and face. His jaw was wider and there was something about his walk.

She couldn't quite put her finger on it, but it was enough to raise suspicion.

"No! What the fuck!"

The slamming of the room's door caused Marlana to jump and tightly press her back against the wall. *Another Jacob.* A second man had entered and quickly made his way to the altercation. The original man, believed to be Jacob, began to turn his body but was suddenly halted. Unforgiving barrels of death were placed on the back of his neck.

"Feels like a sawed-off double barrel of fun to me," Marlana's assailant muttered with a hint of sarcasm as he slightly shifted his eyes to catch the other man in his peripheral vision. "Jacob Ferrell? Is that you? Or am I you? Not so sure any more."

"Marlana, it's me. Get out of here. Now!" Jacob, holding the firearm, commanded.

"He lies! The guy that has this friggin' arm cannon on my head is the one that didn't buy you back from those rogues! Me . . . I was about to kill you. The Council's brainwashing got to me but I think I'm better now. If I were you, I'd get the guards!"

"I'm flattered, quite frankly, to have this much attention surrounding me. But boys, it's got to come to an end sometime. I NEVER told Jacob about the rogues, so catch you later, asshole!"

With those words, she slipped past the men and quickly swung the door open. She proceeded to call for help.

"So . . . " the first Jacob said to the second Jacob.

"Yes?"

"Gonna blow my brains out now?"

"I guess so."

"You know, I was paid by the Council to do this. I got nothing against you or the girl. Lucky for me I was born with such a pretty boy, handsome face, eh?"

"Sorry, but I don't see no black robe, buddy. No immunity for you."

"Oh, well. I tried."

Chunks of flesh, bone fragments, and what seemed to be a gallon of blood made its way to the wall Marlana was previously leaning against, and splattered all over the place like an abstract painting of Jacob's life.

"I'm really getting sick of this shit."

Marlana had reentered the room with Karl and three additional guards.

"What the hell happened?" Karl asked, wearily approaching Jacob.

"Don't worry, it's me. I think . . . I think he learned his lesson well."

Karl squinted his eyes with a small degree of anger.

"Death is not something to make jokes about."

Marlana took a deep breath and smiled. Jacob focused his attention on his fiancée and smiled back.

"Just trying to lighten things up."

"There is nothing to light up, boy."

Marlana turned to Karl but said nothing, despite her built-up aggression.

"Is that blood coming out of your mouth?" he questioned.

"Yeah."

"You okay?" Jacob wanted to know.

"Yeah. It's nothing."

"Okay. Well, Marlana, we got some stuff to do. Maybe you guys ought to go guard the place."

"Whatever," said Karl, giving Jacob the evil eye and signaling for the other guards to follow him out of the room.

Marlana listened for the door to be shut and hurried over to Jacob, kissing him on the lips.

"You taste like blood. Sure you're okay?" Jacob asked.

"Yeah, Jake. It's self-inflicted."

"Right."

"It's a nervous habit that I've got."

"I know, I know. So, you wanna go to Atkins now?"

"Yeah, let's visit the old-timer and then maybe we can have some time to ourselves?" she asked with a hint of playfulness.

Jacob was about to speak and then froze with a look of concern.

"Umm . . . yeah . . . my thoughts exactly. But we might want to remove the dead guy first."

32

The Eleventh Hour of Fucking Reprisal

A dark crescent-shaped shadow formed a sinister half-moon resting on the brim of Robespierre's hat.

"He was a good man," he paused for a moment. "I had to say that, it's customary. Although we hardly knew him—he was a friend to all that met him. A true man of his word. A visionary, if you will. Please, Father, give us a moment of silence for our fallen comrade who has passed on while defending his Empress." Robespierre read a slightly skewed eulogy.

Manfred rested against a tall whitish-gray tombstone that was in the shape of a crucifix. Its paint had grown thin and was already peeling off. Earthworms surfaced to wallow in the newly placed dirt. Shards of flaking paint became stuck to their slimy bodies. Here, surrounded by decay, engulfed in icy perpetual darkness, Manfred's mindset resembled his alleged wandering soul as he found the graveyard to be most fitting. Like a ghost filled with malice for the living, Manfred wished to haunt those that were more fortunate.

"Here lies Manfred Vega. Brother, lover, friend."

Manfred methodically smiled and slowly motioned toward his gravestone like a judge pointing to a convict that was about to be hung. A ghostly aura was transmitted from his body.

"I'll be damned. Someone actually put up the money to have me buried. Well, symbolically anyway. Have you checked the obituaries, Robes? Because I guess I'm pretty dead."

"I know. I'm looking at your tombstone."

Disorderly rows of graves lined the field. Pale moonlight cast a shadow from the men's cigarette smoke onto the head of a nearby remembrance statue. The dark swervy lines gave the memorial an air of enchantment.

"I'm going to put a lot of people down here." Manfred spoke coldly, with a distant look in his eyes. "Soon we will be in the Imperial city of Despair. We're going to see a certain deity that may or may not receive us well, but we will visit her; nonetheless. There, we shall take what we need in order to finish the job. Eleven hours from now will be my fucking reprisal."

He and Robespierre walked slowly amongst the tombs.

"But we will accomplish nothing unless I gain some respect around the capitol. And in order for that to happen, somebody's got to die. A few people have to die."

"Understood. I don't necessarily want to do this—but it's business."

Manfred turned to take one last look at his eternal resting place and then he noticed the inscription on the stone that lay next to his.

"Mollie Weatherbee? Oh, God. Sweetie, I . . . "

The statement took Robespierre by surprise. He opened his mouth to ask a rather obvious question but wasn't sure how to phrase it.

"She was my girl, Robes. I was going to marry her once. And that son-of-no-good-bitch Union fuck killed her on our holy day of matrimony."

Robespierre took two steps back as a precaution to Manfred's sudden change of demeanor.

"Manfred . . . I thought you were arranged to marry her. And didn't care?"

"I lied," he said slowly; his eyes shifting to the ground in shame.

He slightly lifted his head to make eye contact with Robespierre and then refocused on the ground. Manfred simply could not speak clearly any longer. Seeing Mollie's grave caused a burst of sensitivity, that had been lodged deep within his heart, to resurface.

"Listen, I know that I'm breaking character. But I loved that girl. Mollie was my special someone. I mean, she . . . wasn't perfect, but God, did I end up loving her like no other. You know what?" he asked with a warm smile.

"Umm . . . what?"

"I'm kind of sorry I told everyone such a lie."

"Why did you?"

"To save face, as a man to fear. And besides, I'm in love with Marlana. Granted, I guess I did all that I could have with that one."

"Take it easy. It's not your fault, Manfred."

"Yeah. I am what I am, Robes."

Manfred gazed at Mollie's tomb for the final time; his voice was broken up and his eyes glazed over with anxiety.

"She actually used to refer to me as 'her darling.' Fuck, those were the days. Used to keep a picture of her on my nightstand, next to my pistol. Damn. This is not the time to talk about this."

Robespierre patted Manfred on the back and began to speak.

"We all have lies, my friend. For instance, my accent. It's . . . kind of fake. I wasn't born in France, I've never even been to the country—if it still exists," he spoke with an over-pronunciation of his words. "I am a Frenchman—technically. I'm not what you may refer to as a 'poser.'"

Manfred smiled again; this time less emotionally.

"Well, you learn something new every day."

Stepping away from the past, the euphoria had faded from his eyes and raw hatred returned to take its place.

"Shall we get back to business?"

"Yeah. I think . . . I think it's time."

"Shall I alert the others?"

One could see that Manfred was now using the Mollie situation to add more fuel to his already roaring fire.

"Yeah, I'm starting to feel like my regular self again."

33

Stupid Girl

The small woman genuflected to a plastic sculpture of the Blessed Mother. The statue had been painted by hand; it appeared as though its head had been reapplied with Krazy Glue. The woman took a few quick steps over to a pile of magazines and kneeled down facing a wooden cross that was roughly nailed into the wall. A child's equivalent to a teddy bear—a furry purple seal—gazed at the woman with its pale button eyes.

"Shut up, silly-bones. I'm praying for him. Did you know that Jesus loves the little children?" she said raising her voice with playful inquiry. "I don't want to be yelled at anymore, Sunny."

Echidna's face clamped up; she looked like she wanted to cry. Her lips curved downward and a lone tear slowly glided down her pale face.

"I wish . . . I wish . . . " she mumbled, pausing for a moment to giggle. "Marlana was dead. I wish . . . that perfect little angel was sent to hell. Sent to Hell. Love, Echidna."

Her eyes opened wide and she dashed to a nearby mirror. Several small scars were now present as a result of the exploding door at Manfred's wedding. Her cute little face had finally been tainted to match her far more tarnished soul.

"Hmm. It's not that bad. What do you think?"

The seal continued to stare into nothingness. Its button eyes were sewn on just perfect to create the illusion of sadness.

"Don't be sad. I'll be okay. It's not very bad, you know?"

The room's unruliness was breathtakingly morbid. Old newspapers, empty vodka bottles, and crumpled-up pieces of paper were piled in large mounds. The walls, painted a disgusting hot pink, were bastardized with long black streaks of God knew what. Whenever she lost her temper she'd throw furniture. Around the doorframe there was a bloody handprint. An attempt at suicide that had not been a success.

"I like what I have become. Can't say that anyone else will."

A smile of sadism became her dominant feature. Strands of unruly blonde hair hung down, concealing her eyes.

"I made you a finger puppet, Manfred. See?" She chirped erratically as she removed a small plastic baggy from a "Hello Kitty" backpack.

She took out two cloth puppets from the bag and sat down on the floor. She carefully placed a puppet of a rabbit on the index finger of her left hand and a puppet of a bat on the index finger of her right hand.

"I'm lonely and scared," the pink rabbit commented to the bat.

The bat did not reply. Echidna lowered her head and shed another tear. A crudely drawn but vivid picture put together with crayons and construction paper caught her eye. A bluish woman with long dark hair was being stabbed to death by a little pink bunny-rabbit. She smiled; surprisingly not aggressively, but lovingly.

"Yes. I will kill you. And all will be well this Christmas."

Someone knocking at the door interrupted her unstable thoughts. She placed her toys on the ground and started to get up when it forcefully burst open. In came a man in his mid-thirties. He was balding slightly and his stomach protruded below his belt buckle.

"You betta give me my end of shit, ya little bitch."

"Yikes! I will. I've been busy."

The man's eyes scanned the room.

"What da fuck happened here?"

143

"It got messy by itself."

"You gettin' cute with me!" he demanded to know, as a vein projected itself from his forehead.

"I'm not doing anything. Please don't yell at me."

"So. Ya haven't been doing your job?"

"I got fired from the Empire as a 'clean-up' girl. I'm not used to collecting money for a boss."

"What are ya used to collectin'?"

"Fucking heads. Or balls."

The man raised his guard and took a step back.

"Just collect da bills for me, and bring me my money from all dem motherfuckers dat didn't pay up. Okay, little girl?"

"Yeah. But you don't have to be such a meany. Big meany."

Echidna began to cry once more. She picked up Sunny the seal and gently patted him on the head.

"Why da fuck did I hire you?"

"I'll find the people that owe you, Mr. Loan Shark!"

"Okay, bitch. But if you don't . . . "

The fat man's hand quickly encircled Echidna's small neck until he had acquired a formidable grip. He proceeded to squeeze for several seconds until Echidna was beet-red and gasping for air. She clutched Sunny as tightly as she possibly could.

"Do not fuck around again."

With those words he turned and exited and room.

"Probably . . . not a . . . good idea . . . " she gasped.

Her lips curved oddly, expressing an uneasy half smile that abruptly faded, followed by a giggle.

"Silly bones . . . " Echidna moaned, casually reconstructing her grip firmly around Sunny's furry neck.

34

Mama Kutu's

An unknown smell of bitterness engulfed the stale air. The small hut was dimly lit by a rather primitively constructed lantern.

"It is dangerous here, Empress. We really should be leaving as soon as possible," Mina informed her master.

"Don't be foolish—no one even knows that I'm here."

Mina hid her growing concern and quickly walked outside. To her left she read the giant neon sign: MAMA KUTU'S. The "t" in "Kutu" blinked annoyingly off and on. It was a half-way decent place to get a drink and carried the rather 'alternative' setting a lot of customers enjoyed. The bar area was separate, yet attached by a door, to the aged run-down hut. Seventeen Imperial guards and around thirty standard soldiers of varying rank patrolled the perimeter. They were drinking, shouting expletives and being as loud as humanly possible.

This doesn't appear very suspicious . . . she thought, sarcastically.

"Boys . . . you mind quieting down a little bit?"

They put their horsing around on pause just long enough to realize that the person making the request was not the Empress herself and then they continued to misbehave. Feeling a tad stressed, Mina re-entered the hut and gagged. The original stench had been replaced with something most foul. She turned her head to cough and found herself eye to eye with the severed head of a dog. Its eyes had been removed and were replaced with some sort of colored stones—it was suspended by a metal stake that was crookedly protruding from the dirt floor. Small plants grew around its base. Murmuring of an eerie and foreign tribal antiphon was now audible—it was coming from the other side of a beaded doorway. The Empress motioned for Mina to accompany her. She slowly and methodically pushed back several rows of beads and entered the hut's second room.

Wooden bowls, each containing a distinct substance, were strategically positioned around the decrepit surroundings. A tattered woven chair rested in the center of the array. Behind the chair stood an obese black woman. With her back turned to the Empress; she hovered over a large cauldron. Upon the realization of having company she turned, and Mina observed the skull of a small animal as it was suspended around her neck. A brilliantly colored box-shaped hat was removed out of respect and placed on a nearby stool.

"What brings you here again so soon, my daughter? Come for a drink?"

"I need a glimpse of the future, Priestess."

"Let me prepare the recipe," she said as she waddled to a cupboard; one of its glass panels were missing and the other smeared with a mysteriously suspicious maroon liquid.

She began to remove a multitude of items including what appeared to be a human skull. Some other items within the cupboard were jars of fish heads that were freely floating around in preservatives, giant spiders caked together by their own juices, and bags of dirt and sand; each marked with a small note of paper. The High Priestess placed it into the cauldron and chanted a small monologue.

"Priestess Kutu. I take it that there are no cameras in here?"

"No, love. I don't have to worry about the cameras."

"Then I may as well explain my course of action. Mina, leave us."

With that, Mina wearily passed through the beaded wall looking back only once.

146

"A battle is on the horizon and we shall have an opportunity to permanently destroy the Union."

Kutu continued working but kept an open ear to the Empress.

"When that is accomplished, there is little point in keeping the Council around. I'm wondering if, and this is a big 'if' . . . What if we just called the battle off and everyone attacked Council. Bring down their rule. Then, I can conquer the Union and annex it as part of Despair. We'd have to temporarily join forces with the Union. The Council is too overwhelming to defeat on our own."

"My intuitions tell me, love, that a warrior from the opposing side in The Game will take your life beforehand."

The Empress' jaw dropped and she stomped her foot on the dirt floor.

"Who is this warrior?" she asked with a mixture of worry and anger.

"Hard to say. My concoction is not yet to be ready. When it's done I can give you a more accurate prediction of the future."

Kutu heated the pot by lighting some dried-out wood that was hidden underneath. She grabbed a long wooden spoon that was resting on the leg of her chair and she began to stir the mixture in a counterclockwise fashion.

"I order you to come back to the other side of Despair. We need to plan the proper course of action."

"Yes. As you wish, love," Kutu very neutrally concurred and then went on to explain something rather odd. "Leave some of your men—I will follow them back. I must stay until I have finished your business here. There is something . . . that will help you along your way."

The Empress listened intensely.

"I am about to give you something that you must keep on your person at all times."

She removed a corked bottle from her dress pocket. Walking over to the countertop, she snatched a miniature doll that resembled a man holding a rifle and a clothe bag. The Empress took the items and observed the bottle closely. A label that was beginning to peel off read: *Darkest Hour.*

"What is inside?"

"It's for you to find out. You'll know what to do."

"And the rest of these enchantments?"

The High Priestess simply smiled and winked, knowing full well what kind of mischief she had in mind.

"Thank you. I trust your guidance. Certainly nothing but good ever comes from you."

35

Unnatural Selection

A wicked smile revealed clenched teeth. The Man pointed to a small computer monitor. Atkins' bodyguard, Karl, was shaking the hands of two suspicious Union soldiers.

"They're in place. The Imperials, Lieutenant Andrews, and McDaniel are in place."

"Excellent," another Council member responded.

The Man's straggly gray hair created the illusion of madness. As he quickly stood up, three additional monitors mysteriously flickered on to show new camera angles of the event. The other member was astonished.

Telepathy? he wondered.

"Mind your own business."

The Man's mouth did not move a muscle. It never opened.

"Uh, sir . . . I apologize for overstepping my bounds."

Squinting his eyes, he zoomed in to closely observe a small vial that The Man had removed from his robe. He threw the test tube to the ground and covered his mouth with his sleeve.

"No! Sir, what is this?"

"Relax, Number 56. The cure is sitting right next to you."

Number 56 quickly assembled a hypodermic needle and injected a solution into his right arm.

"Now, the big question is, can you read *my* mind?"

"No, but I can take an educated guess. We're going to release this chemical, and only we have the cure," he explained.

Feeling fed up with The Man, his secrets and mind games,

Number 56 attempted to block the frustrations from his brain before they were used against him.

"Precisely. Everyone will be sick and dying, but it's a slow-working disease. We will cure only those who will continue to partake in The Game. All the peaceful ones and troublemakers will be left to die."

"The best part is, I'm willing to bet everyone will blame nuclear fallout."

"Exactly. We won't be linked to this. Except when we distribute the cure, but we can always say that we created it to save their miserable lives from a plague."

"You certainly are a genius."

"Yes. You, however, are not. Granted we do have both the disease and the cure. You just injected yourself with an altogether separate poison a few minutes ago."

"W-w-why? Why did you lie to me?" 56 murmured as his head began to swell with numbness.

"Because I felt like it."

56 fell to the ground and gently slipped into a coma. A thin layer of saliva trickled from his mouth.

"Hmm. He'll snap out of it in a few days. Now, to inform the core to manufacture this by the gallons."

He marveled at the broken test tube for a moment and then gave orders into a nearby monitor.

36

A Messy Situation Involving Blood

"So. Dan 'The Man' . . . how was I?"

"Pretty good. You've been better though, honey."

Suzie rolled off of Dan with playful anger and pulled the sheets over her naked body. Dan placed his hands behind his head and smiled with confidence. This fit Suzie's fancy as she turned to her side and began to stroke Dan's chest hair.

"I'm so glad that we got to stay on Imperial soil, and in Despair of all places! I love it here," she said with enthusiasm.

Dan, never wiping the smirk from his smug face, reached over to the nightstand for a magazine when he noticed that *Kaiser's Revenge* was no longer hanging above the fireplace as he had left it.

"That's odd. Baby, did you . . . "

Remorseless steel tore through the bed and found its way to the other side, protruding from Dan's chest and spraying blood into the air.

"Oh my fucking God!" Suzie yelped and fell from the bed; her naked body came crashing down upon the warm carpet.

The steel slowly slid downward, making its way out of Dan's flesh. Manfred rolled out from under the bed. A few drops of blood stained his gray dress shirt.

"Shit. Now I have to change my shirt before I see the Empress."

"Please don't kill me!" Suzie pleaded. She yanked the sheets to her body to hide her nakedness.

"Why are you covering yourself up? Everyone's seen you naked before."

"You haven't!"

"Always a cute girl. Never too bright, though. I'm afraid I have to kill you now."

Suzie tilted her head slightly to see if Dan was still breathing.

"No, that fucker's dead."

"You should be dead! This doesn't make any sense! Stay away from me you fucking demon!"

"Demon?"

Suzie wasn't sure how to respond. A few tears trickled down her face.

"Ohhh. Don't cry, little girl. I'll let you live if you give me some info."

"O-kay . . . "

"Is Echidna Von still alive?"

"I think so."

"Now that wasn't so hard, was it?"

"No, I guess not."

"See, we can be friends."

Manfred noticed a Council-maintained camera hanging from the wall.

"You hear that they are installing these fucking things into every house now, and in every town square there will be a fucking TV that will show public service announcements from the Council! Cool, huh?"

"Don't speak of such things! They'll come and arrest us!"

"I heard that rumor in the ghetto. I bet it's true though. Think so?"

"I think . . . yeah, possibly."

Manfred tore the camera off of the wall and viciously stomped on it until his foot was sore and the camera was in pieces.

"Dan did that. Not me. Hopefully no one caught this shit on

tape. I mean, hopefully, no one saw it at all. I like being dead and buried."

"Yeah? Psycho . . . "

Even with the threat of impending death Suzie remained as catty as possible.

"But soon, I'll be back amongst the living . . . resurrected from eternal damnation."

"You're very poetic."

"Think so?" Manfred asked with a smile.

Church bells echoed through the small room.

"Hear that? Kind of adds to the drama," Suzie commented.

She stood up and deliberately dropped the bed sheets.

"Mmhm . . . Nice rack. You know I used to have a little crush on you?"

"Yeah, I remember."

"Oh?"

"Still thinking of killing me?"

"For trying to manipulate me with sex. Yeah, actually, I am."

Suzie's face lit up with shock.

"What are you, gay?"

"No, bitch. I just have . . . "

"You're in love with that Union bitch!"

"Not . . . well, yeah, okay."

There was a moment of awkwardness.

"Is there anything I can do for you, in exchange for my life?"

"Well . . . we may as well put your talents to good use."

Suzie strutted provocatively to Manfred and got down on her knees. She unzipped his fly, glanced up and waited for his approval. Manfred was moments away from tossing *Kaiser's Revenge* to the ground when he had second thoughts.

"You know, what the fuck am I doing? You still think you're better than me."

"No, I don't!"

"You do. Admit it."

"No, I won't *admit* it."

He took a step to his right and aligned the blade with Suzie's neck.

"No, you can't be doing this! I don't want to die! You cannot be doing this! You're fucking dead!"

"Well, then, that makes two of us, baby."

Suzie's head rolled underneath the bed; her body collapsed lifelessly, draining red all over Manfred's shoes.

"And now I have to change my fucking shoes, too."

After taking a few quick glances around the room and observing his carnage, he wiped the blood from *Kaiser's Revenge* with the already soiled bed sheets.

"Ahh, good times."

37

Dirty Spies

Dave and Ryan, still wearing the standard Union fatigues that were issued to most low-level soldiers, schemed behind a few parked vehicles.

"Okay. In case something goes wrong out here, that's one hundred bombs in one hundred vehicles," explained Dave. "I got the detonator."

"Shit. Never thought it would be this easy. I mean, even if . . . shit. We deserve some serious cash and prestige, man."

Ryan pointed in the direction of a hollowed-out forest. Rows of Imperial tanks were already beginning to form the frontline of attack.

"Take a look there. Our friends are arriving for the battle."

"Think we better stay hidden back here?"

"Yeah, def."

"Hey . . . umm . . . what if a bomb hits one of these tanks or whatever? I mean the ones we just put explosives in?"

"Christ! We better hope they don't use these trucks until the end of the fight as planned."

Union tanks, jeeps, convoys, and military transports embarked toward the frontline. Officers shouted orders on the placing of each vehicle and soldier as if it were all a giant game of chess.

"You two."

Dave and Ryan were startled and turned to face the unknown speaker. Jacob, with a look of inquiry, motioned for them to come closer.

"Who are you?" asked Ryan.

"You ought to know. I'm one of three commanders that are leading the assault. Commander Ferrell . . . "

"Oh, we didn't recognize you without rank, like on your jacket, man."

"Well, you two better grab a rifle and head over to your lieutenant. We're creating our lines of attack and building our defense. Putting things in order. Things are going to heat up in the next few hours. Hate these Imp bastards."

Jacob nodded his head and walked in the direction of yet another group of idle soldiers.

"Man, I shot that guy a while back," Ryan commented.

"Huh? Oh, in Boston that time. Yeah . . . "

Dave smiled, removed the detonator and handed it to Ryan.

"Go ahead. You can take care of this."

"Umm . . . No. You got it."

"Fine."

"So. If the Union starts to win, we blow all this shit up. The Council will send their own army to temporarily aid the Empire, cause we, as spies, technically violated The Game on the part of the Union? I mean, for all practical purpose, we're Union soldiers right now."

Dave patted his comrade on the back.

"Very good," he said sarcastically. "Just watch your back. You heard the guy a minute ago. Shit is gonna hit the fan."

38

From Sea to Shining Sea

"In your future, love, you shall be the sole ruler of the known world," Mama Kutu predicted while speaking to the Empress with her back turned. "As long as you can survive the not-so-distant future."

She stood in the center of a carved marble balcony that was protruding from her richly built palace. To her left and right, two iron poles with the image of a cross glistened in the blinding sun. Her eyes followed the lines of soldiers marching in the narrow streets. The front row proudly trekked forward, lugging monstrous flags bearing the Imperial blackbird. She observed her domain as an enormous red and black striped banner was draped down the side of an Old World skyscraper. Several small domes surrounded the tall building; she paid close attention to the citizens inside. To her, they were nothing more than mere ants and she, a master entomologist that was researching their predictable but fascinating colony.

"We shouldn't remain out here for too long. The Council will grow suspicious. They always complain when I disappear off camera."

"Yes, love. Do you still have the items that I gave you?"

"I do."

Just then, an Imperial guard stepped out on the balcony and saluted his mistress.

"Pardon the interruption but we have arrested a man claiming to be . . . " he trailed off.

"Just spit it out."

"The ghost of Agent Vega."

The Empress spun around. Her eyes grew wide with the impending threat of the unknown.

"He was with several associates."

"Bring them forward. Bring them all to me, now!"

Confused, the weary guard fetched the prisoner. Kutu winked and clasped her hands together. Her flamboyantly, bright yellow and brown dress seemed to damage the Empress' eye whenever she stared directly at her. A handcuffed Manfred was escorted to the Empress as requested. Two soldiers stood perfectly still, steadying their rifles on Manfred's chest.

"Release him."

The head guard, almost reluctantly, unlocked the handcuffs and allowed them to freely fall to the floor. He took a few steps back.

"Y-y-you . . . " The Empress stuttered in awe.

She moved in closer to Manfred and placed one hand on the side of his face.

"You came back to life?" she asked.

"Yeah, I guess so," he said, refocusing his blank gaze from the floor into her eye.

"Still got the half of veil thing going on. Kinda sexy."

"I put the money up to have you buried."

"Thanks, boss. That's what I figured."

Always fascinated with the occult, the Empress was in her own little paradise.

"Lower your weapons, you idiots!"

The two soldiers that were holding the rifles to Manfred swiftly moved back into the palace as though they were being scolded by their mother and sentenced go to bed without dinner.

"I'm going to conquer it all, Manfred. All of it."

"Yeah?"

"A battle is taking place this instant in which the Union may or may not fall. I suggest . . . " she paused.

The head guard suddenly pretended that he was deaf, turning his head from the conversation.

"The Council. We ought to destroy it. It's too imposing. Make a peace treaty with the Union beforehand . . . temporarily speaking. We'd need them in order to bring down the Council. But then absorb the Union, round up and kill anyone important after we have seized the day."

"Take out the Council? Sounds good, Boss Lady. But, yeah, we'll need Union support, like it or not."

"The Council doesn't enable me to run my government my way. If they even allow a law to be passed, they may or may not change their mind a week later and do what they see fit, regardless. And ultimately *their* general laws for the nation, which are always changing for whatever reason, overrule mine, no matter how much I protest. This system greatly upsets me. Every time something must be done, they send a meddling representative."

"Yeah."

"Whatever the case may be, we shall hold a grand reception. All of Despair is invited."

"When? Now?"

"Soon."

"Will there be booze and women?" Manfred laughed.

The Empress didn't appear to be amused.

"What?" he asked playfully. "Okay . . . my mistake."

"Where are your men?"

"Right here guys, come out here!"

Robespierre and his henchmen, Mick, Chavo, Vicks, and Wedge, entered and proceeded to marvel at the breathtaking view.

"This is Robes. He and his two men, they owe me a few jobs. They will be your personal problem solvers. The other assholes wearing the ugly, red, old-school flak jackets will . . . well, consider them your entertainment."

He paused for a moment.

"Like jesters."

"Very well," she commented.

"Oh, man. Shafted again!" whispered Wedge.

"Dude. No shit!"

The Empress pointed to Vicks.

"Someone kill him."

There was a short stint of confusion. Manfred removed his .22 pistol from under his jacket. Robespierre and company did not hesitate to hold Vicks in place so Manfred could obtain a clear shot. He turned to the Empress and waited for the okay.

"No! I'll do anything! I'll be your personal servant! No, dude!"

She smiled condescendingly.

"I was merely being naughty. They *are* rather amusing. Thanks for the gifts."

"Sure. Oh! Almost forgot. Am I going to jail for disobeying orders?"

"No. I will pardon you for anything you may or may not have done. Consider yourself my bodyguard. And during the ceremony you will function as protection. I hear that there will be an attempt at my life."

Kutu's ears perked up and she slightly tilted her head to listen.

"Who put out the hit?"

"We don't know. Probably someone from the Union."

"Sadly, they think that eliminating you is going to bring righteousness and peace to the world. Whatever. Ultimately, the assassin is probably just another glory hound looking for a bone. Well, whoever this jackass is that wants you gone, just consider me your personal hero killer. Anyone that wants to try and be special will only wind up dead. I promise."

"In the meantime I shall prepare the best course of action in regard to the Council."

Manfred opened his mouth to speak, hesitated, and then began talking anyway.

"Good call. With the Council gone, the Union won't expect a surprise attack later on, if that's what you decide to do."

"You appear to be in agreement with this. Why?"

"I have my reasons. Let's just say the Council's marriage laws always got me a little down," he said with a smile.

"Still having women problems?"

Manfred, quite embarrassed, nervously rolled his eyes.

"Umm . . . no. I'm cool, as always."

"And my last question to you before you are dismissed. I take it you weren't really ever dead. You simply . . . " she mumbled, not bothering to finish her sentence.

"Yeah."

She appeared to be fascinated by this.

"Damn straight I was. I saw the white light at the end of the tunnel."

He smiled and then suddenly remembered something rather important.

"Oh, shit. Where's Benedict? I got to kill that old fuck. Let me tell you something. This friggin' guy is part of the Council . . . " he was cut off.

"I had a feeling you were going to say that. He was an officer that never quite existed."

"What?"

"A computer program. Written by the Council and placed into our own communication systems."

"Fuck that shit!"

"Would I lie?" she asked.

"Delete him!"

"We can't locate the source of his input."

"Wait. So he got the job as an officer and no one saw him?"

"He existed once. Murdered, of course. Replaced by a damned robot."

"Are people still following orders from him?"

"No. I null and void most of his requests."

"Don't worry, boss. Real soon, we won't have to deal with this shit any longer," he barked with anger.

"Correct. We've always made a good tag team, Manfred."

With that being said, she arrogantly turned her back on the crowd and her eyes refocused on the city life.

39

Just Another Old Man

Marlana placed a hand on the old man's shoulder. She was wearing a pair of faded jeans, a white tank top and Jacob's green infantry jacket—he hadn't needed it since the promotion. Sewn into the right sleeve was a nametag reading "Ferrell." She looked sorrowful.

"I always said to myself, if there was a way to end it all, I would. No matter the cost," Atkins explained.

The Union leader sat down cautiously and rested his aging bones in a brown, old-fashioned rocking chair. Marlana brushed back a few strands of long dark hair that had come loose in the breeze from an open window.

"I'd give anything to end the struggle that almost took my life. The same struggle that caused Jacob to nearly kill me."

"Sometimes your boyfriend worries me. He seems programmed. He wants to defeat the Empire first, before furthering any plans," Atkins stated glumly. "We must unite the sides. Word has it that some people within the Empire are even considering it."

"The Game will come to an end. That is my dream, that is the only way for *all* of humanity to exist in harmony, absent from this death and decay. And in order to end The Game, the sides must unite and then take on the Council's government. There is no other way that we can assure victory—one side could never defeat the Council alone."

"Personal vendettas have to be overlooked, at this point. If one side destroys the other, the survivors will be too fatigued to fight another war against anyone. One faction can never attack the

Council directly, without making peace with the other side, because the other side would still probably continue The Game regardless. The Council is very powerful and we'd need all the support we could get to even come close to taking it down. And besides, will the Council ever let The Game die?"

"No."

"This will be harder than you think. There are still citizens that will not let The Game end. Remember that. People you trust . . . even love. It shall be up to you, Marlana, to put a lid on this can of evil."

"W . . . why me?"

"Soon . . . radiation poisoning will take my life. I've done all that I could."

"Oh, God! I'm so sorry. I don't know what to say," she said with dismay.

"It's in its early stages. I still have some time, but not much."

"This comes as a rather horrible surprise. I'm not sure what I can do alone, without your leadership."

"I'm just another old man. Convince Jacob to help."

"I will."

"When I die, he will take my place as leader of the Union. It'll be your job to make sure he does what is right."

The breaking news didn't have much time to settle when the door swung open and in came Karl.

"You wanted to see me, Atkins?"

"Yes. So you think that it can not be done with the current Empress in power?"

"Absolutely not. She's a power hungry maniac. She'd never give up her seat of control when the time comes to form a unified government. So I need your approval before I can go through with what we discussed."

"If you feel that this is the only way, then do it."

Marlana turned to Karl and studied the man's stern, nearly expressionless face.

164

"Umm . . . Karl . . . what are we talking about here?" she asked.

Karl made eye contact with Atkins until he received the "okay" that allowed him to proceed.

"I hired an assassin to take out the Empress. If we want to unite the factions, she's got to go. She'd never agree to an idea like that, and we can't just run it by her for the hell of it. If the Council finds out, they'd kill us all."

"Our intent must remain hidden for at least the time being," Atkins added.

"With her gone, maybe someone from the other side will listen."

Marlana cringed at the thought of endangering the destruction of The Game.

"What the fuck, Karl? Maybe the Imps won't make peace with us if we kill their leader. For Christ's sake!"

"Calm down, I've been doing this for a long time. I know what I need to do. Thank you," he retorted bitterly. "He's freelance. A fucking rogue. The Imps won't know who put the hit out—could have been anyone."

"Fine, then."

"I'm going with him. I plan on disguising myself as a peasant and sneaking in. I have people on the inside and I can ask if they heard anything about the Empire considering calling it quits."

"People know you, asshole! You're going to fuck it all up!" Marlana yelled.

"Oh, I didn't know that you were a military strategist," he spoke with anger.

"Everyone calm down. It'll be okay. This is what must be done," Atkins wisely interrupted.

Marlana lifted her brow, folded her arms, and turned her head in disgust. For some reason, as much as she despised confrontation, there was something about it that made her feel important. Something that gave her a certain satisfaction from the

165

attention that she always received.

"I know what needs to be done. Whatever it takes . . . " she mumbled. Then she realized suddenly that she, almost eerily, reminded herself of someone.

40

Violations

Droplets of cold morning dew clung to the helmet of the wounded soldier. He tilted his head to reveal the source of the dim shadow that was being cast over his dirt-ridden face.

"No . . . " he whispered pitifully.

He crawled backwards. His mouth hung open in awe. An inhuman presence returned the acknowledgment. Wearing jet-black fatigues and a dark helmet that was attached to a gas mask, an operative drew a large handgun from his belt. Tubes ran from a tank of oxygen to the bizarre soldier's mouth area; the sight of flesh was intimidatingly not visible. The fallen man attempted to peer into the large, cold glass eyes of the gas mask but could not make out a single human feature. Bone fragments and chunks of flesh exploded as a result of the slow drawn-out pull of the trigger.

"Yet another lawbreaker eliminated," an amplified, half-muffled voice spoke.

Hundreds of these soulless militants patrolled the damned field of broken concepts of hope. Union and Imperial vehicles lay scattered throughout the dry sullen meadow. Some were abandoned and intact, others badly damaged or engulfed in flame. The deceased were still and the injured quivered; they squirmed and pleaded but to no avail. Watching the carnage from behind enemy lines, Jacob put down his binoculars and turned to a nearby soldier.

"What the fuck? The Council has their own army? I knew it," he mumbled.

"Sir, they appear to only be killing *our* injured. Why?"

"Violation of The Game. I don't understand it. We were doing unbelievably well and then there was a God-awful explosion. By our own people, I guess. Someone detonated a bomb that must have been planted earlier. This is the result," Jacob remarked sadly.

"I think, sir, that we were going to actually pull the upset victory . . . before the sabotage."

"I'm going to get to the bottom of . . . "

Before he could finish his sentence the deafening humming of airplanes zoomed past their heads. They were dumping gallons of what appeared to be a green mist.

"Christ! Some sort of chemical weapons! Cover your mouth!"

Jacob kneeled down and coughed into the sleeve of his jacket.

"Gas masks . . . no shit."

"Sir, do you think that the Council," he stopped to think and then continued, "but it's hitting everyone?"

"Yeah. It is."

There was a brief pause.

"They're infecting us all."

41

Rival Teams

During the extended duration of waiting for her new employer, Echidna required a change of clothes. A cotton skirt and navy-blue top were roughly removed and tossed to the floor of the room in a small building. She released a large sigh and shrugged her shoulders. Echidna had returned to Boston for the odd job of collecting money for her lone-shark boss. Things, as expected, spiraled out of control. Two more dead people to add to her ever-growing list of hapless victims.

Better not get caught.

Murdering members of the same faction was illegal, of course. Echidna figured that if she altered her appearance a bit, she could slip away without being seen. That was probably her most rational thought of the year. The sudden rumbling of the abandoned building caused her to freeze instantly. In a state of panic, she dashed outside and witnessed three airplanes soar by, all dumping chemicals.

"It's pretty," she giggled.

"Yo, bitch. Why you almost naked?"

It was her boss. Echidna, still in her little pink bra and panties, bent down, seized a medium-sized stone from the sidewalk, and whipped it at the man's skull.

"What da fuck?" he yelled as he removed a handgun that was tucked between his belt and fat gut.

Echidna was as perplexed as he; she had no firm understanding or justification on her behalf. He felt his forehead and moved his hand closer to his eyes to view a patch of blood. Before the man could fire one round, Echidna charged him and booted him in the groin; she achieved possession of the firearm, and ended his miserable existence with one well-aimed shot to the throat. For reasons unknown, she pulled the trigger until the clip was empty.

"Ha!"

She waited for a response of some sort, and then had the revelation that her ex-boss was soon to be pushing up daisies. Echidna threw the gun to the ground and danced her way to the man's car. Popping its trunk and snatching up his baseball bat (She knew it was inside because she was previously threatened by it. "Don't fuck around," he once said, pointing to the bat.), as violently and as aggressively as possible, Echidna attacked the car as though it posed a legitimate threat. Chips of orange paint and glass flew in all directions. She smashed the windshield like it was going out of style, and she laughed heinously as she did so.

"Oooh!"

Manfred was confused. He didn't have to actually say it. The priceless look on his face said, "What the fuck?" better than the actual question itself. A small blonde girl, in her underwear, no less, annihilating an inanimate object with a deadly weapon. *How would anyone react to that?* Echidna carefully dropped the bat. The moment of truth had arrived. Her eyes lit up with blind happiness and her jaw dropped. A perfect smile appeared for the first time in a long time. As quickly as possible, she ran to Manfred and embraced him. She held on to him like grim death as Manfred forced a smile and put his arms around her. One of his hands slowly slid up her bare back. He gently stroked her hair out of friendly admiration. Subconsciously, his fake smile transformed into a rather warm sentiment.

"My love. We missed you!" Echidna exclaimed, burying her face into the man's shoulder.

"Yeah. I'm kind of glad to see you too, honey," he softly spoke; he was beginning to catch himself.

He gingerly took a step backwards. Not enough to prevent further touching, just enough to establish a greater sense of casualness.

"Huh? Come over here. You're not happy to see me?" she asked. "It certainly *felt* like you were!"

"Well . . . you are almost naked. And I always thought you were kind of cute."

"What? I meant . . . "

She smiled and touched his face.

Oh, shit.

She extended her arms to the back of his neck and pulled him closer. She moved in for the kill. Her lips were a mere inch from his. Manfred did everything in his power to not make eye contact, and then, all was lost. One small peck quickly turned to three and continued on until Echidna gently pushed him onto to a nearby park bench and positioned herself on top of his lap.

"Whoa," a random passerby commented on his way to work.

"Manny, right now!"

"Wait! Jesus Christ!" he exclaimed.

Manfred squirmed away from Echidna and stood up. A look of angst dominated her face.

"We shouldn't. We're professionals. I came to Boston to ask if you wanted to re-join me."

"Yes."

"I heard that you were a little lonely without me? Thought I was dead, eh?"

"No . . . I just thought you . . . abandoned me," she glumly mumbled, giving Manfred the puppy dog face.

Echidna lowered her head sadly and Manfred could tell that she was losing interest in making a comeback. He reached forward and pulled on one of her pigtails, in hopes that it would spark some interest. Playing with the tips of her hair, a slight expression of superiority came over his face. Manfred leaned closer and then strained himself to appear concerned.

171

"I wouldn't do that. As fucked up as you may be, and as much of . . . a bastard as I may seem, I wouldn't forget about you, kid. I'd never do that. Besides, I got more work for you," he spoke in a forced, uncharacteristically calm voice.

A bit of her initial happiness had returned and she quickly perked up, not even questioning Manfred's manipulative ways.

"Come on, E. I got something to show you," he said as he pointed to a large building; a neon sign read FLEETCENTER.

They walked indoors, up a small flight of stairs, and over to a concession stand.

"No one has been here in quite some time. The roof leaks. Got hit by a stray Union warhead."

"Manny, what's this?" asked Echidna.

She had located a box with some sports propaganda. Opening it up, Echidna was very pleased with her findings. She began to dress herself by sliding a green-and-white cheerleader skirt up her legs and roughly tossing on a faded wrestling T-shirt; the image of a skull and bones was ironed into its center. She tied the bottom of the black shirt into a knot to expose her bellybutton as a pair of work boots caught her eye. Manfred stuck his hand in the box and pulled out a Boston Red Sox jersey.

"You know, Echidna, they used to hold sporting events here."

"I heard."

"Two teams competing for glory. Or money. Yeah, money. Kind of like our Game, but there's less of a point to that."

After switching shirts, he leaned against a vandalized wall and lit up a smoke. The verse "Yankees Suck" had been spray painted behind him. He pointed to the graffiti.

"That was the rival team to the Sox. The Yankees. You got to admire the passion. I mean, someone was so pissed off at our rival team that they fucking sprayed that on the wall. It so reminds me of us, and what we're expected to do and shit."

"Umm. So, Manny, did you convert Marlana to the Empire? I know that was something that you wanted to do."

"No."

"Still want to?"

"Maybe. Yeah, I guess I do. Fuck it, might as well keep trying. I have nothing else to think about. How could I get her to join? If she did though, at least our conversations would be legal."

"I shall do what is required of me then."

"Yeah?"

"I guess so. I mean, if she crosses me, I'll kill her, damn it. But otherwise, I will respect your wishes, my love."

"You're a good kid. We should head back to Despair soon."

"Despair?"

"Yeah. Apparently we have work that needs to be done."

"Fun, fun . . . "

Manfred took one last drag from his cigarette before he tossed it.

"For my own selfish reasons, I think I'm going to promote the destruction of The Game. To kill the marriage laws. I still got plans, E."

"Whatever. I'm hungry. Let's go find something to eat."

Normalcy, if one could even use that word properly, had returned.

42

Doing the Right Thing

Twelve men and women waited impatiently for the meeting of Union minds to begin. They encircled a large wooden table headed by Jacob Ferrell.

"We're in Portland today for one reason. I called for this meeting because someone from the Union put a damn knife through *all* our backs and sabotaged The Game," he spoke with authority.

"Jake, Atkins is sick and couldn't make it. I guess that leaves you in charge, but let me make one thing clear. We must respect his wishes. When I go to Despair tomorrow, I will find someone to listen to our plea," Karl explained.

"What's our plea?"

"Can't say right now, for reasons that you know about."

"I know what Atkins always wanted," Jacob said, turning to a camera that was mounted on the wall. "To abolish The Game. But it can't happen yet. Not now. So, Council, you don't have to worry. I hear that the people that detonated those bombs were actually Imperials! Big surprise? Not one bit."

"It's true. Spies. Two of them. They were under the aliases of Jon Higgins and L. MacDonald, two deceased men. They . . . disappeared," a Union general informed the crowd.

"Well, we better fucking find them."

"Listen, Jacob, I understand your anger with the Empire but . . ."

"They can all go to hell. The Empress, Kutu or whomever.

174

Find me the damn Imperial spies. With Atkins out of the game, no pun intended, I'm the acting minister of the Union. I'll tell you what to do. Forget the Council, for now. The Empire needs to be defeated first."

"I sort of agree. But it's not all your decision. The Empress needs to go, but . . . well . . . nothing further," Karl responded nervously. "Things . . . could be worked out. I mean, with someone else in control of Imperial forces . . . "

"No. Unfortunately, it will never be worked out. I'm not saying certain things shouldn't be done *in time*, but the Empire must be destroyed first! I won't say it again."

"What about the Council infecting us all with a disease!"

"Yeah? And if we fight The Game they will cure us in time. That's the purpose of the airplanes and the gas. I know! It's their plan. Think about it!" Jacob exclaimed as he pounded his fist on the hard wooden table. "Go along with it and they will fix that mess on their own. Fight the Empire and be cured. They can't let us all die! Only those that choose to not take up The Game. Why go against the Council if we will all die anyway? I know that I don't have a cure, and won't get it until certain things happen."

"They're going to kill us all! Or at least, most of us, damn it!"

Karl stood up and shouted into the camera.

"Fuck this!"

Jacob angrily gritted his teeth and objected to Karl's uproar.

"Shut the hell up before you get us killed for sure!"

About half the crowd appeared to be pleased with Jacob and the other half leaning more toward Karl's point of view.

"I'm sorry that this is what it all comes down to."

"Just worry about your end of shit, and I'll worry about mine," Jacob threatened.

"Listen. We will eventually have to make peace with the Imperials," Karl responded, slowly. "And with that being said, I'm about to get the hell out of here before the Council shows up, looking for me. If they want me, I'll be in Despair killing the Empress. They won't interfere with that."

With a look of dismay, Karl quickly dashed from the room, nervous about the commotion he had caused. As soon as he was out of sight, Jacob addressed the others.

"First things first. I'm going to do what I think is right. The Empire and the people working for it are corrupt and deserve to be reprimanded for all they have done to us."

No one said a thing.

43

The Parade

Smoke poured from battered dilapidated skyscrapers, decorated with Imperial propaganda, and polluted the misty night sky. Hordes of humanity donated their falsified sense of pride, waving and cheering as the Empress' remote-controlled platform trudged through the dark streets of Despair. Rows of scantily clad dancer girls, covered in tribal paint, wove between men spitting fireballs and performing magic tricks. Every female dancer wore a purple or maroon veil that had an extended tail that twirled around their bodies as they moved. A regiment of highly trained soldiers marched behind the brilliantly decorated platform. Lines of burning torches guided them along the way, while seedy henchmen were scattered on watchtowers, peering through windows and wandering the street, silently awaiting conflict.

To the Empress' left and right were Imperial guards, protected by high-powered assault rifles and thick body armor on their torsos, knees, and elbows, relentlessly keeping an eye open for suspicious activity. Robespierre and his goons slowly scanned the crowd for any sudden movement. The Empress, herself, rested on a magnificently carved wooden throne. Directly next to her was Mina, sitting on a stool, leaning over to whisper suggestions. By the Empress' personal request, High Priestess Kutu is in the crowd, cloaked with a brown hood, hiding on the outskirts of the celebration.

A man sporting a lengthy black leather coat, and his wired sidekick guarded the front end of the contraption. Manfred coolly leaned against a speech podium, and smiled at the small inscription of a blackbird.

"When I told you to change your shoes, I didn't mean for you to put on another pair of boots. I like the cheerleader skirt. You know, a lot of teenagers find the cheerleader look sexy," he explained.

"Only silly Billys would walk off with a guy wearing black leather, and a Boston Red Sox jersey," she said, sticking her tongue out. "You're not looking for a hooker later, are you?"

"Shut up. Well, at least Empress Gustav looks hot tonight. The fancy headdress thing works for her. I'd like to lift up that veil sometime, and see if she fixed anything."

"You should. Wait . . . fixed?"

"Echidna, never mind. I mean, there's a reason why she wears it. That's all I'm saying."

"Think so?"

"I know so."

"Hey, whatev. Manny, why do I feel like we're hired goons?"

"Because we are. Important hired goons though. I mean . . . yeah, 'whatever' indeed. This sucks. I want to find some action."

"Thinking about trouble, my friend?" she chirped with a giggle.

"With whom?"

"Maybe Jake and Marle will show up?"

"No way. They're too high and mighty for that now. We'll never see them again."

"Yeah. We have to."

"Why?"

"Because."

"Alright, I don't even want to hear it, because I know what you're thinking. You still want to kill her? I told you . . . she's not your business anymore."

There was a slightly awkward silence before Echidna decided to break it.

"Manny, we're a lot like a tribe, you know?"

"Yeah," he said, barely paying attention as his eyes focused on a female dancer.

Just in his field of vision, several rows of tanks and jeeps rode in from a side street and began to maneuver to the back of the parade.

"Oh, shit. There they are. I was wondering where the rest of the military was."

"Duh."

"Duh?"

"Yeppers."

"Echidna, shut the fuck up."

"Okay," she said with a vibrant smile.

Manfred slowly came to the realization that he returned the sentiment once more. A warming sensation filled the pit of his stomach.

"Something wrong?"

"Must be something I ate."

Before Echidna could respond, she recognized a potential problem.

"Oh, shit. Look! It's those guys!"

"Son of a bitch."

He couldn't have been more pleased.

"Go take care of it, kiddo."

"You betcha."

Echidna jumped off of the moving platform and disappeared into the crowd.

Karl, wearing a hooded sweatshirt and disguised as a civilian, peered through the barrel of a sniper rifle.

"See her?" asked his associate.

"Yeah, that is her. But so what?"

A rogue gunman, also undercover, was hired to take the fall for the assassination of Gustav. Karl handed back the man's rifle and shook his head.

"But she's a master of black magic."

"You don't actually believe in such bullshit? Out of all the bad-ass mercenaries I get Little Bo Peep."

"I'll do it anyway. But I'm just saying, you know."

Karl clutched the man by the shirt.

"You better do it."

"I will! But why is this so important?"

"Why do you think?"

"Alright, alright . . . "

He released his grip on the sniper and leaned against the wall.

"Here's the deal. When you get the absolute best shot, kill her. If she don't die, then I will have no choice but to charge the stage, along with several others that are positioned in the audience."

"Sounds more like a cry of desperation than a plan."

"Just do what we paid you to do."

"I just want you to know that the second I shoot, I'm out of here."

"Fine."

The rogue pressed the butt of the rifle firmly into his shoulder.

"Okay. I'll be waiting for her to come around."

"Fair enough."

Karl took a moment to ponder if the rogue was reliable or not and then walked down a flight of stairs and into the vast crowd. Out of the corner of his eye he saw Echidna Von whiz by in quite a hurry. He quickly pulled the hood of his sweatshirt tighter around his face; this caught the attention of Kutu. She noted the watchtower that the unknown man had exited from and decided she better personally warn the Empress. The Priestess, feeling there might be a serious threat, decided that if she was the bearer of urgent news, then certain prophecies would appear more accurate. After allowing all potential danger to pass, Karl found refuge behind a few soldiers and silently anticipated chaos.

Ryan and Dave, dressed in Imperial gray, were taking a smoke break inside an empty watchtower. Motioning with the gumption of superiority, Ryan pointed to the ceiling, in this case, a representation of the sky, and smiled.

"It's begun. And we'll be the first to have the cure, buddy."

"The Council will drop that shit and man . . . we're in good graces with the true rulers of the known world. The best part is, we're back on Imperial soil! Home! And no one expects a thing!" he exclaimed, releasing a puff of smoke.

"How many guys can honestly say that they were in a Union city for over twenty-four hours? Huh?"

The duo slapped each other on the backs and laughed exuberantly at what appeared to be nothing. The tower's door slowly creaked open, but in their excitement, neither individual took note.

"So, where's Dan and Suzie at?"

"No clue. I haven't seen them since getting back."

"Hello, friends."

Both men abruptly spun around, discovering nothing.

"What the fuck was that? Someone else in here?"

The light switch was flicked off.

"Jesus Christ, man! Turn it back on!"

A girlish giggle filled their eardrums with impending insanity.

"Oh . . . you got to be kidding me . . . "

Without much thought, Echidna slit the first Achilles' tendon she could find.

"Oh, God!"

Ryan collapsed to the ground and experienced the agony of a jackknife being slid into his throat. When he was gasping for air, choking on blood, and violently squirming, Echidna was a happy little girl.

"Fucking bitch!"

A hand viciously seized her foot and yanked her to the ground. Echidna leaned forward and swiftly worked on the knot in her shoelace. Dave suddenly found himself holding the shoe of a schoolgirl.

"I got new shoes from the shoe store. They're only twelve minutes old. See?"

He angrily tossed it to the ground and took a swing at Echidna. She landed on her side and bruised her cranium; her skirt fell back, exposing her panties.

"I'm not sure, bitch, if I saw that right, but you are wearing the same style of shoe my kid sister wears!"

"How old is she?"

Dave stopped dead in his tracks. He nervously checked on Ryan.

"Come on, buddy. Don't die on me!"

Ryan attempted to respond but a knife in his voicebox prohibited him from doing so.

"Please just stop, lady!"

Echidna grew sad and stood up. Her mouth curved downward and she began to cry. She stomped her foot on the ground one time and her whimpering vanished without a trace.

"Huh?"

"Daddy never let Echidna play fair."

Echidna dashed over to Dave and jumped on his back. He desperately tried to shake her off, but not before she snatched the knife from Ryan's throat. She jabbed it into Dave's chest with gleeful delight. Both people came crashing to the floor with an enormous thud. Echidna's mental state was inexplicably saturated with a deep burning rage. She crawled on top of Ryan's quivering body and pressed her two thumbs into his open wound. Inserting them into his neck, she patiently waited till no oxygen reached his brain.

"Die, daddy, die!"

Her eyes glazed over with neverending derangement. Ryan's murmuring faded to silence, and Echidna lay still on top of his lifeless body. Breathing hard, a treacherously cold smile was plastered across her otherwise innocent face.

Feeling the slits that he had cut into his jacket so that *Kaiser's Revenge* could rest on his back, a wave of content for the new look caused him to grow weary and he decided to wander around.

"Empress, I'm going for a walk."

"You stay here."

Manfred's boredom had reached an overwhelming pinnacle. He waved to a few people he had never seen before, and then sat down on the edge of the moving platform. He let his gaze wander until he came across a familiar face. A harsh flashback to the after-effects of his impromptu wedding ensued. Karl also recognized Manfred and gritted his teeth with anxiety. The time for hesitation was prematurely over. Karl pushed a man from his path of motion and drew a good-sized machete from under his sweatshirt.

"And I thought you were just happy to see me."

Manfred quickly unsheathed his katana and deflected Karl, knocking him down. Civilians mauled him with whatever they could but Manfred, surprisingly, protested. Three soldiers surrounded Karl and raised their rifles without further thought.

"No! Wait!"

For reasons unknown, Manfred gave the orders to back down. Robespierre and the Imperial guards seized the Empress and attempted to deliver her to safety.

"Put me down this instant!"

Manfred took a few steps forward and placed his blade against Karl's throat.

"Why'd they send you to kill her?"

"I came under orders from Atkins, but it's not what you think!"

"Then what the fuck is it?"

A citizen removed a pocketknife and nonchalantly walked in front of a soldier.

"We want to make a treaty that will end The Game!"

"Holy shit . . . "

Manfred took a deep breath and listened to all the bickering from the audience. The citizen lunged forward and motioned to slice Karl's back open when Manfred swiftly changed the direction of his sword's blade and took a mighty swing into the man's abdomen. Karl was in complete disbelief. *Maybe they were going to listen to logic after all?*

"Take him away, he's my prisoner. Someone contact the Union and tell them we have him here. They'll have to send their leader to speak with ours on the matter?" he asked, raising an eyebrow to his Empress.

"Yes."

As Karl was being placed in handcuffs, a bullet from an unknown shooter grazed the upper thigh of the Empress. She abruptly collapsed to the ground, then was yanked to her feet and dragged to the rear of the platform. Soldiers boxed her in, waving their rifles in the air; prepared to die for their mistress.

"Find him, now!"

Six or seven men exited from the sea of humanity and bolted toward the stage. Manfred's revolver had returned for the first time in a long time. Sadly, for him, he never had the chance to pull the trigger. The army made short work out of the assassins. Only one Imperial was even wounded during the brief shootout. Manfred ignored the citizens' cheers and coldly waited for a second wave of assault. He got nothing.

Suddenly, a bullet from the sniper dropped a guard that was standing next to Gustav. The soldiers that were on the platform scanned each watchtower with intensity; not knowing who would be killed next. Like clockwork, three more soldiers and one Imperial guard collapsed. With each bang, bullets rained closer and closer to the Empress. Taking a clear shot at Gustav was becoming easier with less obstruction. Frantically, Imperials in the street began to attack all visible watchtowers, without the concern of friendly fire. Gustav reached under her dress and searched for the items that Kutu had given her a few weeks ago; they had vanished.

The High Priestess was fully aware of the shooter's location. Standing in front of the watchtower, she firmly clutched a doll that was shaped as a man holding a rifle. Opening the small flask entitled "Darkest Hour" and pouring a foul-smelling liquid on the doll; she revealed a collection of pins. The rogue gunman, so very close to accomplishing his mission, was now facing a most troubling variable. Beads of sweat poured from his brow; his aim badly tainted. In order to take out Gustav he'd have no choice but to eliminate this menacing distraction. It would be impossible for him to concentrate with the irrational fear of voodoo. Kutu maniacally slid a pin into the doll's hand.

The rogue dropped the sniper rifle and clutched his left index finger. It felt as though it had been snipped off with a pair of pliers. By now, the Imperial guards had located the shooter and stormed up the watchtower's staircase; however, when they reached the assassin he was already lifeless. An expression of intense fear was burnt into his face. Outside, resting next to Kutu's foot was the doll; three pins protruded from its chest. The Priestess laughed, knowing full well that her credibility had risen dramatically. Echidna was hiding behind a small building; she timidly peeked around the corner. Her mouth hung open and her eyes grew wide with the horror of the unexplained.

"She earns her paycheck," commented Manfred.

"Indeed she does," Gustav responded. "So, it's over now?"

"Yeah. But how did she know where the guy was?"

"You do not think that she foresaw it?"

"She foresaw it alright . . . she foresaw a bigger pocketbook."

"Manfred, that is not your concern."

"I know. Sorry."

Echidna, screeching as she ran, unwisely startled Manfred; she grabbed his coat and pulled him closer. Hugging him with force, she did not let go.

"I'm scared!"

"What's your problem?"

Gustav, observing her subjects, shot Manfred an icy dagger with her one free eye.

"Yeah. Sorry, E, come here . . . " he unwillingly muttered.

Manfred returned the hug.

The Empress placed a hand on his shoulder. Echidna walked to Gustav's left and awaited orders; Manfred remained on her right.

"We will hold Atkins' man as bait for a meeting."

"Sounds good to me."

There was a short pause in dialogue.

"Think Kutu just knew where the guy was? I mean, like no special powers? She just knew and didn't tell you so she'd be the one to take him out. With 'magic' no less. So, it raised her credibility and her earnings?"

"Silence. Agent Vega, when will you learn to keep your mouth shut? Mama Kutu is creditable enough," explained Gustav.

She took a deep breath, almost having second thoughts.

"It was a psychosomatic-type deal. The guy was just that scared of the unknown," whispered Manfred.

"Huh?" Echidna loudly retorted.

"Just never mind."

The Empress turned her head and faced Manfred, then Echidna.

"We'll shut up now, boss."

The second she had removed her attention from the infamous duo, Manfred whispered it again.

"Psychosomatic . . . "

44

Another Conspiracy

"What should be our darkest hour will prove to be a valuable lesson for us all," The Man commented.

Resting on a steel chair and rubbing his head to clear his thoughts, The Man glanced through some documents and surveillance photos.

"We have visuals to confirm Agent Vega is still alive," a number informed his superior.

"He won't be for long. I know this for almost a fact. Later this week, the new Union Minister, Jacob Ferrell, along with his fiancée, Marlana Von, will be holding a meeting with Empress Gustav in regard to discontinuing The Game."

The conversation transpired in a Council Headquarters; a large ominous building that held records and information on the population. The structure was surrounded by barren desert; a result from the War of the Old World. The sand itself was poisonous, and thus Council members often suffered from radiation sickness. A minor flaw in the system, the lower numbers chose to ignore the situation rather than admitting a mistake. Temporarily leaving the core, The Man had traveled there in order to discuss business with underlings.

"And what of Atkins?"

"Fortunately, he died a few hours ago. Radiation poisoning. Forget that. We shall have no fear of The Game ever coming to an end. Unnatural selection has begun and anyone that doesn't play will not be cured. Trust me. They know this. Could they be so foolish as to defy the hand that will cure them?"

"No, they will not. Where will this meeting occur?"

"In a small buffer zone between the lines referred to as the 'Abyss.' We have spent recent funds on installing TV monitors with audio capability into all town squares and many private homes. Instead of broadcasting live feed to a Council control center, we shall send the signal to the citizens' monitors. This meeting and the action that follows will be on live 'television.'"

"How can this even be done?"

"The Council's core building has a super-transmitter. A computer we have there is fast enough to import feed from an Old World satellite, which will collect the initial input from the cameras. We'll just have to pay close attention to Vega—I'm sure he'll do something worth broadcasting. Wherever his crimes may take him, we should follow. Even after the meeting, eventually events that will promote The Game are inevitable. If not, we'll deal with that."

"And what if they come to an agreement? With all due respect, couldn't it backfire?"

"It won't because they will not agree on anything. We will take the appropriate measures to make sure that won't happen. In the Abyss, there is a town and a functioning train station. We have already designed a train bearing the Imperial Blackbird that will hold a large explosive. Train tracks from Abyss connect to the Union town of Kittery. We will make it appear as though the Imperials concocted a trap."

"I see. What if no one responds because they expect citizens acting on their own accord? There is still plenty of animosity on both lines. People may consider that a possibility."

"I already thought of that. The facility that we are in right now, our second largest headquarters, will be approximately thirty miles away. I'll remain here and use my mental superiority to manipulate one of the players that I know will not hesitate to cause a problem."

"Echidna Von?"

"Yes. Such an interesting girl. A perfect citizen and player in The Game. We can also use the Ferrell-Vega conflict to our advantage. They will inevitably go after one another. We will broadcast the winner killing the loser. This will further disunite the sides."

"Amazing."

"Something you want to say?"

"Don't you already know?"

"Yes, and if I were you, I'd be impressed by me as well."

"But there are a few minor issues."

"What?"

"Many people have grown upset with us. We have evidence to back that up. They're talking about us. They are upset with the chemicals being dumped. Perhaps we rendered a problem?"

"Silence! What kind of talk is that? We are superior. And I do not care who is angered by our actions. They won't be saying anything when it's time to distribute a cure. Just as easy as they can call for a meeting to end The Game, we can reinstitute our power like nothing even happened."

45

Congregation in Abyss

It had been raining for hours and the faint scent of ozone filled the air. Karl wiped the sweat from his brow and leaned against the thick metal bars of his holding cell. A five-o'clock shadow tainted his stern face. His brown hair was unruly. He cracked his neck and placed his hands on the cold steel.

"There he is. Unharmed as we promised," Gustav stated, waving her left hand in the direction of the cage.

She was surrounded by Imperial guards, soldiers, politicians, and henchmen, minus her two favorites. An uneasy tension polluted everyone's thoughts. This was the largest congregation of neutrality in ten years. Despite popular belief, there were no physical signs of the Council except hundreds of cameras that had been recently installed throughout Abyss, most likely in the anticipation of this particular event. For reasons unrevealed, a large television monitor was mounted on the wall.

"So, did we understand each other? He's to be let go!" Jacob demanded.

There were a handful of Union soldiers and supporters in the midst of what appeared to be Imperial supremacy.

"Don't push your luck, Commander Ferrell. He'll be set free after we come to a decision."

Marlana leaned forward and put her arm around Jacob.

"How touching."

"Can we just get down to business, Empress? And I'm saying that with all due respect," added Marlana.

"Fine then. You don't leave such a bad taste in my mouth as your boyfriend. Explain your position."

"I will. I wish for The Game to be abolished. If we all say 'screw it,' how will the Council reprimand us?"

Suddenly, Marlana's face appeared on the room's monitor. (After she had finished bad-mouthing the system, of course.) Whispering broke free amongst the crowd until the Empress could stand no more.

"Be quite. Everyone!"

"Hey! You can't order me around, lady," Jacob said rudely.

"I can do what I please."

The camera angle had switched to Gustav.

"We're being televised."

"Anyway, we all know that the Council has infected us with a slow-working poison. I say we hold off messing with them until we are cured," explained Jacob.

As expected, Jacob was now on television. Wherever he was, The Man probably wasn't pleased with Jacob admitting that the Council was behind the infection; however, things were now moving smoothly in their favor. Marlana experienced a sharp pain in her lower stomach. Nausea, quickly followed by a headache, prohibited her from countering Jacob's dialogue. She was under the impression that the Union would be disagreeing with Gustav, but not complying with the Council. She didn't have much of a warning when it came to the outburst of conformity. Biting her bottom lip as hard as she could, Marlana removed her arm from Jacob.

"No! How do we know they'll cure us? If we continue to fight this war we'll all die anyway!"

Jacob was stunned and appalled.

"What? Marlana, not now, honey."

"Shut up, Jacob! Empress, it was Atkins' final wishes for a unified America. I vowed to end the fucking Game at all costs," she stated, firmly.

Her eyes narrowed with seriousness.

"We agree. And how do you think this should be done?" Gustav questioned with a hint of intrigue.

Jacob was beside himself.

"I'm the boss here. Don't listen to my girlfriend! She's not herself today!"

Karl turned his head in disgust.

"Whatever. Just . . . we can have two separate countries if that suits you better, Jacob, but we must stop fighting!"

"Yes, two countries would be better for us as well. But peace is all that we truly desire . . . " Gustav mumbled.

"Fine! Then screw it! Let's get a treaty going. We'll see what kind of a deal we can come up with."

The insincerity in Jacob's voice was enough to convince Marlana that she had a new problem on her hands. A problem that she had no idea how to resolve and still manage to walk away happy.

"Our goal is to concoct an arrangement to nullify every rule the Council has ever imposed on us."

Marlana nodded her head in agreement. She smiled at the Empress, who did not return the sentiment. Just then, the back door swung open and Echidna stumbled wildly inside, almost tripping over herself.

"Guards! Restrain her!"

"W-w-what the hell?"

Three Imperial guards motioned for Echidna to leave the room. She reluctantly turned around and scowled.

"Fine! I'm going! Stupid!"

"Guards, stay by that door, if she comes back; kill her."

"Yes, Empress."

For her sworn enemy, Marlana certainly didn't mind the Empress. Echidna tried to listen in on the meeting by pressing her ear against the door. Her head grew numb and she felt the necessity to sit down.

Your sister . . .

"Who was that?"

Marlana...

She pulled at her hair as her eyes glazed over with fluid. "What . . . what about her?"

Kill her...

Echidna, not that she resisted much, was experiencing a burning desire to re-enter the room and murder Marlana despite the almost certainty of death. A sea of voices rushed into her cranium. She stood up and placed her hand on the doorknob.

"I just can't help myself. Here goes . . . "

She froze.

"Oh my! I almost forgot! I bet my cupcakes are done!"

Overcoming her mysterious urges, Echidna happily sauntered in the opposite direction and began to walk down a flight of stairs. Not even looking back for a second, she had bypassed an attempt at Marlana. This time, oddly enough, perhaps her mysterious impulses, which would normally be natural for a disturbed girl like Echidna, came from another source. A source that used mental telepathy just for fun. Nonetheless, Echidna gave the situation no rational thought; after all, she was easily distracted.

Back inside, Jacob angrily shook the hand of the Empress. He tightened his grip and squeezed with force.

"This better not be a double cross."

"I wouldn't dream of it," she said.

Out of nowhere, a stray bullet bounced off of the back wall and entered the midsection of a Union soldier.

"Oh shit!"

The Empress drew back from Jacob.

"Wait, no one do anything!"

Vicks elbowed Wedge in the stomach.

"Why'd you do that?"

"I was nervous, man. My finger slipped."

By this point, the soldier was lying dead, surrounded by very upset comrades.

"Which one of you idiots fired that round?" Gustav demanded to know.

A small line of smoke ran from Wedges' rifle.

"The jester?"

"We're not really jesters. We're actually con artists. And we've used guns . . . "

He was cut off by Jacob.

"Did you see that? A treaty can't be made with these people!"

Marlana recognized Wedge and Vicks with a sensation of dread.

"No! Those assholes are mere criminals! They have nothing to do with this."

"Men, arrest those two," ordered Gustav.

An Imperial guard placed handcuffs on both "jesters" and pushed them, one at a time, toward the room's backdoor.

"Let's go, jerks," the guard commanded.

"Not fair!"

"Wedge, you moron!"

Gustav silently waited for the disturbance to cease.

"I demand that we make an agreement!" the Empress exclaimed.

"You demand? Fuck this!"

"Jacob, show some respect or this won't work!"

"Marlana . . . "

"You got something to say to me?"

"Yes. We're leaving," he said as he pointed to the room's large double doors that were located at the front end. "I can't take this anymore!"

"Jacob, no!" she begged.

"Men, let's go. This conversation is over."

The Union soldiers wearily followed Jacob to the doors. Marlana sadly trailed behind, desperately trying to think of a plan to accommodate both Jacob and the Empress.

"Commander Ferrell. Despite my wishes to make peace, if

you walk through those doors, I cannot promise you a safe journey home."

"You don't own this place!"

"Just for the record," she said while gazing into a camera.

The Empress' face appeared on the monitor.

"No Imperial is to attack a member of the Union for the remainder of the day. Unless their names happen to be Ferrell or Von. Now, that's an arrangement that should fit me nicely."

Her face quickly disappeared from the monitor. The camera angle had switched to the angry mug shot of a disagreeable soldier, but it was too late and the damage had been done. Powerful orders to every Imperial in the known world had been delivered by Gustav's very own lips. She used the Council's own method against them, without losing face and not allowing the brazen Jacob to walk away a free man. The Council sent a raging blare of distracting static through the lines as an attempt to muffle voices and censor whatever they could. After a few seconds, the room's audio had returned and Jacob became the focused image.

"If that's the way it is, then . . . "

He didn't finish the statement.

"Open the doors. Someone open the doors!"

"If you leave . . . well, you'll have to see for yourself."

"I'm prepared for the worst," he responded as his men pulled the large double doors open.

He tilted his head forward and opened his eyes as wide as possible. Manfred stood in the door frame. His emotionless face said it all. Cracking his knuckles, his mouth curved upward and his eyes grew narrow.

"This is not happening, " Marlana whispered.

"I've been taking too many bullets lately," he mumbled, with a diabolical smirk.

Marlana, already fairly close to the Empress, dashed behind her and placed a handgun to the back of her head.

"Someone free him!"

A guard hurried to Karl's holding cell and unlocked the door. He grabbed Marlana by the arm and they exited through the back-door.

"No one move a muscle."

Gustav demanded silence.

"As I said. To keep the peace, only kill those with the last names of Ferrell or Von."

A horde of Imperial guards, followed by Robespierre and his men, immediately pursued Karl and Marlana. The Union soldiers awaited Jacob's orders, but to no avail; he never made eye contact with a single one of them.

"Manfred! You're alive?"

"Enough with the pissing contest, tough guy. Come over here so I can kill you."

"And you make it sound like you're the good guy. And I'm some kind of dragon that needs to be slain by a fucking knight!"

"You . . . you just stole one of my lines, buddy."

"This time, I'm going to do the right thing and watch you die before my eyes, you scumbag!"

"You friggin' boy scout. Come get some," Manfred said as Jacob tackled him, pushing him from the doorframe.

Gustav motioned for the double doors to be shut. The Union soldiers, although confused, did nothing. They were tired of fighting, and by the look of things, there was no need for further bloodshed. All they desired, at this point, was to take a break from the constant violence that was their lives. The Empress turned to the nearest camera and walked in front of it. She gently touched its sides with both hands and gazed into the circular glass lens.

"The rest is up to all of you."

46

Jesus Saves

Marlana, after reaching the bottom of the staircase, ran outside and slammed the door with malice. With their pursuers gaining ground, Karl desperately scanned the area for some sort of means to create a barricade. He noticed that they were in a train station and spotted a forklift used for loading cargo.

"Marlana, get out of the way!"

Karl turned the key until he heard a mechanized roar. While putting the vehicle in reverse, the door had swung open. Switching the gears to forward and then using the steel lifts as a battering ram, he steered the machine toward his intended target. Before getting a single shot off, three Imperial guards were speared and the entrance was blocked by debris. On the other side, Robespierre and what was left of the would-be assault squad stopped dead in their tracks. Returning to the Empress and delivering the message of failure was an impossibility. Robespierre, now completely soiled, and highly annoyed, instructed his men to clear the rubble. He thought of the jesters and didn't wish to share the same fate. Chavo and Mick took a few lazy steps back and let the others do the heavy lifting. Instead, they began to aimlessly wipe the soot from Robespierre's suit.

"Shit, Karl."

Hopping down from the forklift, Karl pointed to the train and motioned for Marlana to follow him.

"We got to get the hell out of here. This train leads to Kittery. I know that for a fact. Come on!"

When the two had reached the train they were bewildered that it was oddly decorated with the Imperial logo.

"What the . . . ? Should we get on?"

"I have no idea. No idea what the hell to do right now."

Two Council representatives stepped out from a cargo door and spotted the intruders. One of the hooded men glanced in the other's direction.

"Marlana Von?"

"Yes. Rule breaker. Kill her immediately."

The Council members revealed standard-issue machetes and approached Marlana and Karl with a degree of arrogance.

"Jacob!" she pleaded.

"And I thought you were the independent type," Karl mumbled sarcastically.

Choosing to ignore something that she couldn't quite comprehend, Marlana took a few steps backward until her ears were pierced by the noise of someone leaning heavily on a horn. A worn down, crudely painted yellow bulldozer was accelerating into the parked forklift. With her newest distraction, she didn't even have the time to properly address the matter at hand.

"What the . . . Karl, look out!"

He spun around to catch the arm of a Council member, preventing his head from being split open. Marlana removed a hand pistol from under her shirt and blasted the hooded figure through the head. Karl, using all of his strength, charged the other and forced him back into the train. He pulled at the number's hood and positioned his head just outside the cabin, allowing Marlana to slam the cargo door, which now functioned as a deadly weapon.

A small crew of men poured from the hole in the wall like bees leaving their nest to confront a predator. Karl and Marlana took cover behind some wooden boxes.

"Whoever is in the bulldozer freed those miserable bastards!"

Bullets were tearing the wood to shreds. An arm suddenly seized Marlana from behind and pulled her upright. She relaxed her body and used her weight to catch the attacker off balance. He was instantly killed by Imperial bullets.

"He wasn't dead?" Marlana wondered as a dark hood slowly slid back, revealing a pale white face.

The Imperials temporarily ceased their attack when they had realized what had happened.

"Don't stop! Fire!"

After repositioning themselves for further engagement, the bulldozer plowed through the center of the troops and altered its trajectory, aiming for Marlana. Flesh and bone fragments hung to the dozer like ornaments on a Christmas tree.

"Holy fuck, get out of the way!"

Marlana and Karl jumped to the left and right respectively, clearing the dozer's path of destructive motion. The heavyset vehicle smashed through the train's cargo door, rendering itself trapped in the tight-fitting structure of the enforced doorframe. The back end of the vehicle crudely protruded beyond the walls of the train; it poured smoke and leaked valuable gasoline. The driver attempted to put the dozer in reverse but the tracks had been intertwined with large shards of twisted metal. Only a small section of wooden door remained intact and was quickly shot to pieces from the inside. Judging from the amount of rounds fired per second, it appeared to be an Old World machine gun.

"Echidna . . . "

Jacob sadistically wrapped his hands around Manfred's neck and pushed him inhumanly against the wall. The cameras had changed their trajectories and focused on the struggle. Out of the corner of his left eye, Manfred noted a small window. Booting Jacob in the lower extremities, he soared to the glass panel and saw himself on a large monitor that was located in the center of town. Jacob, catching up to his foe, took a brief moment to take in the bizarre sight of himself on television.

"So, Jake, how do I look?"

"Like a dead man."

Jacob threw a right handed punch that Manfred blocked and countered with a knee to the groin.

"I'm going to make sure you can never have kids."

"How the fuck are you even still alive?"

"Shut up," Manfred commanded arrogantly as he kicked Jacob in the side of the head, followed by a short but distastefully sinister laugh; foreshadowing the degree of evil that was yet to come.

Manfred dropped a quick knee to the groin once more, followed by several punches to the lower ribs. Jacob opened his mouth to speak but Manfred silenced him with a fist to the jaw. He applied pressure to Jacob's throat and mercilessly lifted his eyes to one of the cameras, expressing nothing but pure malice. Releasing his grip, Manfred rose to his feet and unsheathed *Kaiser's Revenge.*

"On a different day, I would. Not right now. This Game thing has got to go first."

Jacob, ignoring Manfred's somewhat selfish attempt for good, quickly tackled his opponent and kicked *Kaiser's Revenge* across the room. Manfred retaliated with an eye rake and swift uppercut. Jacob spit up some blood and fell backward, banging his head against the floor.

"Now, I'm going to leave you here. I have something to say to your girlfriend."

"Fuck you."

"Okay. Of course. Actually, now that you've detained me, I have something to say to you too. Why even bother to be everyone's hero? Why even try? They're just going to turn their backs on you the second you don't agree with them. Which is not too far off, by the way. You still want to do what you think is right? If you just let me be, we probably wouldn't even be trying to murder each other. Now who's the bad guy? Still think it's me?"

"Fuck you . . . "

"Some hero. You, not me, are going to keep this war going.

You people are all the same. For your own personal glory you'll kill us all. And you always do it for some girl. I can be a real bastard, but I'm still not willing to step into your shoes. And if I were you, I'd stay put, because when I'm around; heroes die young."

With that being said, Manfred spit upon Jacob's fallen body and hurried along to the cargo area.

Imperial forces had uncovered a large sit-down Gatling gun that had been left over from a war that dated back to the previous century. Once displayed in the town square, it grew rusty and was considered an eyesore. Most likely it had been auctioned and was waiting to be shipped out. Instead, a soldier malignantly turned its heavy crank, spraying bullets and creating clouds of dust as another aimed its enormous barrels. For a brief moment, Marlana envisioned herself being blown apart from this vicious onslaught. She followed her basic instincts and sought refuge inside the train.

"She's in the train. Aim for the train!" Robespierre ordered; the bullet shells were beginning to collect at his feet. "Shoot the . . . "

His speech abruptly ended with a wave of nauseating shock. Four Council soldiers, wielding high-powered modern weaponry encircled Robespierre. Eyeing one of the commandos, he came to note that he was wearing a backpack and carrying a flamethrower. A protective metal face mask concealed his identity.

"Do not shoot the damn train," one of them hissed though the voice amplifier on his helmet.

"Don't shoot the train!"

"What? I can't hear you!" the Imperial asked, continuing to turn the crank.

The Council, without any reservation, opened fire. If he were still alive, the soldier probably would have wished he had had his hearing checked at his yearly physical.

"Now order everyone to enter the train."

"Well . . . everyone else, enter the train!"

Robespierre shrugged his shoulders and reluctantly waited for additional orders.

"That is all."

He took a deep breath and motioned for Mick and Chavo to come closer. The Council pushed him aside and moved in the direction of the train.

"Follow these bucketheads. Make sure the job is done for the Empress. I'll catch up with you gentlemen at a later time," he said, wearily.

"Yeah, if you want."

Robespierre turned around and jogged toward the hole in the wall that they had come from, apparently seeing enough for one day. Having no desire to leave Marlana, Karl simply found it hard to follow her into a situation that included imminent death. Running to a docking elevator, he stepped inside and pressed the button that was labeled with a downward arrow. Taking a glance beneath and looking through the floor that consisted of thin metal bars, he nearly choked on his own saliva. An Imperial was holding a compact rocket launcher. Pricey weapons like that were rare on limited resources. It must have been Karl's lucky day.

"Aim down there!"

He didn't even need to lift his head to see who that was. He swiftly ducked underneath the elevator's control panel and covered his ears as a rainstorm of bullets sprayed the area. The slots in the grated floor were large enough for the bullets to pass through, and the Imperial holding the rocket launcher was a mere second away from pressing the "fire" button when lead collided with the tip of the missile. A furious explosion pushed the elevator back to the main floor, slightly scorching Karl's bare skin. Sucking up the pain, he rolled out from the blackened control panel and pulled the trigger until the clip emptied. A score of Imperial soldiers lay dead, and this generated some concern for Robespierre's thugs. Chavo jumped into the scalding hot loading platform and raised his gun to the back of Karl's neck. He bolted from the elevator to stable ground and spun around just in time to witness the melting gears snap, sending the giant hunk of steel plummeting several stories.

"One down."

Mick cracked Karl in the side of the ribcage with the butt end of his rifle. Karl collapsed backward; his head was now gushing blood. As he was turning his weapon around for the kill, Karl lunged forward, grabbed Mick by his shirt, and tossed him over the side of the newly created chasm.

"Useless goons."

Unfortunately, there was no time to take a breather; Karl was surrounded by a division of Council soldiers.

"Raise your hands in the air."

He angrily obeyed. Now in an extremely foul mood, Karl gritted his teeth in disgust. Even during times of extraordinary pain, Karl could think of nothing more than fighting till his last breath on Earth. He planned on staying alive just long enough to take down one or two, no matter how much lead they pumped into him.

"You're not the primary target. Von is, but we'll eliminate a threat whenever we see one."

"Wait! I tried to kill the Empress! Remember?" he barked while dramatically raising the volume of his voice.

"What's it matter now?"

Karl closed his eyes for a brief moment and pondered the best possible way to keep breathing oxygen.

Echidna knew what her sister knew. Four inches below her skirt, two little red bows decorated the tops of her white stockings; she unfastened one of the ribbons and tied it into her hair, creating a third pigtail. Within the train, directly three cars down, Marlana hid under a scruffy seat cover. She could hear the small pitter-patter of footsteps. Echidna opened the car's door with tender ease and she scanned the room for Marlana; no luck. As she paid close attention to a mirror's reflection of the bunny rabbit on her bright pink T-shirt, Echidna was about to move along but then noted that a camera was pointing to a red seat cover with a human-sized bump in it. Coming to the conclusion that the camera's focus was tipping her off, she grew excited and raised one of her pigtails above her head in a moment of triumph. With a crazed expression etched into her face, Echidna freed a clip for her machine gun that was wedged between her thigh and stocking.

"Uh-oh! You were never very good at hide and go seek," announced Echidna.

"W-what's that on your face? Chocolate frosting?"

"I had cupcakes for lunch today!"

Marlana threw the tarp over Echidna's head and crawled across the floor as fast as possible. Echidna, temporarily blinded and having no patience whatsoever, emptied the clip on the entire room, like it was her versus the train. As she was approaching the car's power box, Marlana finally understood exactly what kind of a maniac she had been dealing with. Instead of messing with "normal sociopath Echidna," she was now messing with "psycho-bitch Echidna." The second form had a definite plus and minus. Clearly Echidna Version 2 is more destructive overall; however, Version 2 could not make a rational decision if her life depended on it. By now, Marlana had this narrowed down to a science.

"Fucking bitch," Marlana yelled as she cracked three of her knuckles open while trying to smash the power box.

She took a look at her hand; blood drained from her open wounds. Before Echidna managed to reload, she wound up and slugged the box once more. This time the lights faded to black and Marlana stealthily crept to the back end of the car. The box's only light source was entering through scattered bullet holes. Echidna was dumb enough to stand between two of them. With limited vision, Marlana removed a handgun and aimed to the best of her ability.

"Bye."

Almost as though she somehow knew, Echidna took two steps to the right and opened a random wooden box. Marlana wondered if her sister even remembered that she was engaged in a deadly battle. She would have gladly taken a shot into the darkness, but she decided to wait; wounding Echidna would only make her more rabid.

Marlana impatiently waited for three solid minutes as Echidna rummaged through items. Beads of sweat poured from Marlana's brow and trickled down her face, running into her mouth. The salty liquid tasted so good; Marlana hadn't eaten all day and was beginning to feel lightheaded. The room grew silent. All that could be heard was the faint dripping of blood. A cold shiver ran down Marlana's spine as her breathing increased. *Tick, tock. Tick, tock.* Marlana had picked out the ticking of her wristwatch's secondhand. It stoically carried out its life sentence of perpetual motion. With each passing second, her situation became more and more uncomfortable.

"*Prrrrr . . .* "

"What the . . . "

"*Prrrr . . . ppprrrrrrr . . . prr . . . vrrrrrrrrrrrrrrrrrrrrrrrrrrrrrrrrr!*"

"Holy shit!"

Echidna had apparently found a chain saw.

Marlana wisely decided to make a run for it. She dashed to the closest door; locked. Spinning around, hair flew in her face. Marlana screamed as loud and as pitifully as she possibly could. Falling to the ground, dropping her firearm, and sliding along the mahogany until her bottom dragged across the floor was a sad way to die.

"You leave me alone!"

"What?" Echidna yelled over the loud purring of the chainsaw.

She leaned forward and mutilated a seat for no apparent reason. Bits of foam and debris bounced of off Marlana's face; she flinched, blinking her eyes.

Is this it?

The burning scent of gasoline filled her nostrils. The chain saw's motor choked for more fuel until it abruptly turned off. Echidna, obviously not pleased, lobbed the tool onto Marlana's leg. The blade scraped a small line of flesh away.

"Oh, Jesus!"

Echidna, without hesitation, slapped her sister and then placed a hand on both of her cheeks.

"I said a prayer you'd die today. Jesus saves."

She pulled her face closer. Echidna's eyes grew wide as though she was under the influence of a foreign substance. Her mouth twisted and turned; she was having difficulty even expressing her sickening impulses.

"Fuck you, Echidna. Just kill me. If you're going to do it, just do it!" Marlana screamed, fiercely.

"Always have to act important. Right to your dying breath."

"Manfred will murder you when he finds out that you've killed me!"

Marlana confused herself and took a brief moment to analyze what was just said. Her sudden need for a man that she despised bore a hole through her thoughts.

"You think he's some sort of hero? Last time I checked, he was a killer of heroes. He wouldn't save you, silly bones."

"Shut the fuck up! How many honest-to-God good people has he killed? It's all hype."

She let go of Marlana's face and entered a state of bewilderment.

"No one, I guess, maybe . . . "

"Exactly."

"I don't know . . . "

"He's not that bad," she mumbled. "I can't say I respect what he stands for but your friend . . . maybe he's not so horrible."

"Huh?"

"I mean, at least you know what to expect from him. Can't say that for everyone. One minute they've got your back, and then they don't."

Marlana had used Echidna's attention deficit disorder to her advantage once more. While distracted, she stuck her thumb into Echidna's eye, applied pressure, and continued to squeeze until liquid oozed out.

"No! Owwww!"

Echidna collapsed in pain. Standing up, Marlana repeatedly kicked her in the ribs. Thinking back on the kidnappings and attempts on her life, she totally lost control. Marlana seized Echidna's head and rammed it into the still blade of the chain saw until her moans and pleas faded to a slight murmur. Her brief moment of sadism ended when she was alerted by booming gunshots. Dropping Echidna, Marlana crawled along the floor, feeling her way around in the dark, until she located the car's door. She peeked outside.

"So, what do we do now?" asked Karl.

"I guess you get on this train and leave. But you're not taking the girl or that deadbeat that's passed-the-fuck-out upstairs."

It was her favorite pain in the ass. Manfred was like a compulsive habit that just wouldn't go away; not even with the proper therapy.

"I don't even know where the girl is."

"Just hand her over. I'm not going to hurt her. Seriously," he said, holding a gun to Karl's head. "Now . . . find her!"

Marlana opened the door as Manfred's head turned to see what the noise was.

"Good. Okay, I just want to talk."

"It's okay, Karl. Get on the train. I'll deal with him. I know he won't hurt me."

"You sure?"

"Like you have a choice. He's got a gun to your head. I'll stay here. This train goes to . . . where's it go?"

"Kittery."

Manfred lowered his .22 and Karl cautiously moved inside the train. Its whistle blew, startling Marlana; she lost her balance and stumbled over a motionless body. She looked down and realized that Manfred had recently slaughtered five or six Council operatives.

"Damn. "

"Like that?"

"Even with a good shot, I know you're out of bullets by now."

"So?"

Marlana laughed sarcastically.

"So what do you want from me now?"

"I was thinking . . . we both want this Game thing to end, right?"

"Yeah?"

"Why not be friends?"

"Because I know that you have more in store for me."

"What makes you think that?"

"Are you serious?"

"No. But, I love you . . . " Manfred admitted unwillingly.

"I don't love you back."

"You never gave me a chance!"

"It wasn't meant to be! Sorry! You're a persistent bastard, I'll give you that!"

"How do you know what was meant to be!"

Manfred sulked his shoulders and appeared to be greatly distraught.

"So, you going to kill me now?"

"No. I wouldn't hurt you. You know that."

Her eyes awkwardly wandered around the room observing the death and destruction.

Was this all a result of one man not getting what he wanted? Or is his love that strong? Or maybe this is the fault of those that choose to follow their own ideals of right and wrong, even if it means all of . . . this.

"Your intentions are good, but I'm sorry."

"You know Jacob isn't dead."

"You kept him alive?"

"For you."

"What kind of a sick gift is that?"

"So want him dead now?"

"No!"

"I hear that lately you don't know what you're going to get with that guy. Didn't I tell you he wasn't forever? I'm not going anywhere, baby."

"I know that."

"What the hell?"

"What?"

"Why did you stay with me? And not get on the train?"

"I wanted to talk."

"You love the attention I show you. Because you don't hate me. You just don't want to have relations with me. Okay . . . "

"I can't. It's too messed up now. It was illegal for us to have pleasant interaction. I mean, that was a fucking law. Can't say that I completely don't like you, if that's what's bothering you. As fucked as that may sound. I should despise you. I mean, I used to, but not now."

"So, what's this mean?"

"What's what mean? I'm sorry, but I'm not feeling it. Besides, I have someone who loves me. Yeah, I do."

"Okay. You know, I feel burnt. And that's why I do the things I do."

"Good for you. Who cares?"

"No one, I guess."

Marlana was shocked to witness Manfred's change in demeanor.

"There'll always be a little place in my heart for you, kiddo."

"Just fuck off. Enough is enough."

The alleged villain scratched his head and wondered if he

had gotten it all off his chest.

"I'm going to go now. Because I've had enough."

"That's ironic, Manfred. I should be the one saying that."

Manfred turned to leave but didn't see an exit.

"Stick 'em up, asshole."

A bloodied Jacob had returned. His face glowed with a never-ending irrational hatred and his finger, of course, rested inside a rifle's trigger guard.

"Jacob, don't! He was about to leave!"

"Thanks, Marlana. You're more concerned over this prick than me?"

"I knew you were okay."

"I'm not fucking okay!"

Manfred closed his eyes and honestly tried his best to keep his mouth shut, but as usual, this was an impossibility.

"You're right. You're not okay. You look like one of those guys that bring a gun to work and go postal."

Marlana, anticipating her boyfriend's actions, attempted to calm him down.

"Don't. You're the better man, Jake."

As the train's engine roared and its wheels began to move along the track, a smile appeared and graced his bruised and battered face.

"Go. You'll miss your train."

Jacob lowered the rifle.

"Only because my girlfriend said so."

Manfred nodded and waited for the couple to move toward the train. He bent down and his hands gently wrapped around the base of a flamethrower that a Council solder had dropped. Thinking to himself, Manfred wondered if he should pull a fast one or just walk away and live to fight another day. He couldn't help himself.

"Jacob . . . You gotta go."

Before anything could happen, Echidna leaped from the train

and cracked Marlana in the side of the head with the butt end of her machine gun.

"E? Kill the guy, please."

"I know, I know!"

Echidna placed the firearm to Jacob's chest, but was knocked down by a fierce punch to the jaw. Manfred threw down his weapon and charged Jacob. They viciously wrestled along the ground; both men trying desperately to tear the other's throat out.

"Your war created me, Ferrell, your fucking war!"

Shaking her head and retrieving her weapon, she waited for Jacob to position himself on top of Manfred and then fired a burst of ammo. This carried on every time she had a fair shot. Clumsily, her timing had been off and bullets grazed the back of Manfred, tearing his jacket.

"Son of a bitch!"

Jacob, using this to his advantage, stood up and kicked Manfred a few times in the ribs and abdomen. By now, Marlana regained consciousness and wrapped her arm around Echidna's thin little neck until she turned blue and fainted.

It was too late. They had missed the train.

"Marlana, let's go to the town square! If we follow the train tracks, I believe the train runs right through it."

"And we want to go there why? Remember, people are trying to kill us!"

"No one can touch us out there. It's neutral territory," he said as he pointed to the light at the end of the docking bay's tunnel.

"I don't know if that will stop the Council."

"We have transports waiting to pick us up, okay?"

"Fine! Then let's get the hell out of here before this asshole wakes up . . . " Marlana trailed off; she booted Echidna in the torso for good luck and then turned around to walk away.

Having an uncontrolled urge, she took a step backward, leaned over and wiped the chocolate frosting from Echidna's mouth.

"You're such a child."

"Forget her. And what about the other one?"

"Him? He's nothing. Harmless. Now, let's go. I assume our people will get us out of here. I want to settle things with the whole Game issue, but apparently now is not the time."

"No, no. Apparently not. Let's go."

Manfred moaned as the couple hurried along. He spit out a small wad of saliva and blood.

"Harmless . . ."

Imperial backup had finally arrived; however, they were no longer needed for anything important. A medic helped a wounded man to his feet and another began to collect leftover firearms. Angrily closing his eyes and clenching his teeth, Manfred took a moment to reflect.

Ignored again. Even now.

Two soldiers stood in front of Echidna's limp body. In their possession were electrical prongs and handcuffs.

"We can't have someone like this wandering around. She's gonna kill us all. Like, maybe even *us*," one soldier explained to the other.

They bent forward and double-handcuffed the blonde. The second soldier jammed his electrode into Echidna's back, sending a small current of electricity into her body.

"Wow. She's out cold. Probably pure exhaustion. Well, that was just in case. Let's take her to jail."

"Yep."

Manfred opened one eye just in time to witness the abuse. Out of everyone, an immature psychopath that was sort of cute, in her own way served as the only person that he could completely put any faith into, and seeing her being played with, deeply enraged him. Marlana, out of the clear blue, had reentered his thoughts for the one-millionth time. For some reason, he still cared for her, but now understood that he could never have her. Manfred had never been known for dealing with problems like this very well. Closing his hands until he could hear his knuckles crack, he wondered if there were more to life than beating people up, getting beat up, and cheap women.

47

All or Nothing

Karl took a deep breath and rested his head against a cushioned seat. Remembering the earlier confrontation with the Council, he decided to check out the conductor's car and see who was driving the train. He turned the metal knob and gasped. A Union soldier rested, leaning against a control panel.

"Don't even think about it, man. The brakes have already been cut. Ain't no stopping this thing," he said with a sigh.

The man appeared to be defeated. His eyelids sagged and he spoke with pessimism. Between the greasy hair, fingernails that were caked with dirt and the unhealthy tone of skin, Karl quickly assumed he had been someone's prisoner.

"Be thankful you still have your own thoughts. They took mine away," mumbled the depraved man as he pointed to a ball and chain that was attached to his leg and a metal pole.

"Who put you here and why? I thought this train was a neutral convoy? Why's the Imperial logo on it? Think we'll get attacked?"

Karl asked as many questions as possible.

"The Council. Who do you think? We got a massive bomb underneath the floor panel that we're standing on."

"No way!"

"Yeah. To get The Game going. They're going to frame the Imps when this thing goes off in Kittery."

"Why the hell are you going along with this?"

"They cuffed me in. But I can't say I didn't originally volunteer. My family gets reimbursed when I die."

"It . . . it doesn't matter. We have to separate this bomb from the train!"

"How? It's in the damn cockpit! It's not like we can detach a car."

"Think if we both lift it, we can throw it out an opening?"

"Don't know how big it is, or if it can be moved. You'd have to get something to pry the hatch open."

The conductor got up and trudged across the room until Karl could hear the clink of the ball and chain restricting his movement. He bent down and felt the metal panel that rested on top of the hidden explosive.

"But we could try. I mean, if it blows up. Then we die anyway. Who cares? Or I certainly don't."

"How big is this fucking bomb? It's going to take out a city?"

"Some of the city."

"Okay. I'll go back into the main part of the train and see what I can find to lift the panel."

"I'll be right here, man."

"Alright."

"Oh, one thing, before you go, do you have any idea what's slowing us down? Someone put cargo in here?"

"There's a bulldozer sticking out of one of the cars."

"Oh."

Karl felt his way around the poorly lit train until his eyes met up with a crowbar. As his grip tightened around cold steel he could feel the equally chilling presence of someone spying on him. A cold sweat poured from his top lip. He shivered in suspense and his pupils grew wide with an irrational fear. A miniature representation of himself had been pinned against the door by a kitchen knife; the doll was nearly sliced in two.

The Man placed two fingers on each temple and used his brain to achieve a sense of their plan's progression. He was able to

215

feel the surprising presence of three individuals. According to his scheme, only one should be onboard that train. Making the assumption that the unknown variables were lawbreakers, he decided to create an unequal playing field. Located deep within the second largest Council facility, between Abyss and Kittery, The Man concocted a solution to this potential interference.

Yanking the doll's head off with his right index finger and thumb, Karl aggressively opened the car door only to find himself face to face with Kutu.

"That's what I figured. I don't buy into that voodoo junk," Karl said with a forced smile.

"I actually didn't expect you to, love."

Kutu pulled a revolver from under her gown.

"What a copout. You're going to kill me with that?"

"Just admit my presence frightens you."

"Yeah. It has nothing to do with magic, though. But I can see why the Empress kept you around."

The Priestess delivered a coy smile.

"I'll see you later, love."

"Wait! Before you pull that trigger I have something to say! This train has a bomb on it!"

"They'll say anything to avoid death."

Kutu began to squeeze the trigger. Karl squinted one eye and gawked at his potential murderer with the other, anticipating the worst. The door behind Kutu flew open and the conductor stumbled inside; ball and chain in hand. The metal pole that was previously restraining his freedom dangled from the rusty chain. A cold and distant look was directed and burned through Kutu, so she opened fire, only making contact three times. Not having a great shot as it was, one bullet was even deflected off of the large steel ball. For reasons that could not be currently explained he continued moving forward like a demented zombie; thus Kutu had become trapped in between the two men. *What was giving the conductor his will power?*

He dropped the ball on her left foot and brushed her aside. Karl took a few steps toward the conductor as Kutu screamed bloody murder in foreign tongues. He struck the man in a bullet wound and proceeded to whack at his body with the crowbar. Insanely enough, this didn't appear to slow him down any. He clawed at Karl's eyes, scratching his face. Karl swung the crowbar and spilt the man's head open like a watermelon. Ignoring Kutu and running as fast as possible to the conductor's car, Karl had the mysterious urge to jump off the train. So he followed this inexplicable desire by exiting the conductor's room, sliding open the next car door that he came to, and leaping out. He landed hard and rolled for a few seconds along the desert floor. After briefly crawling around and spitting some sand from his mouth, the bizarre control over his thoughts vanished. Although he was in too much pain to move, Karl came to a grim conclusion. Someone had manipulated him and the others. The question of "how?" he could not answer. There was no time to even think, and even if there was, he had no patience left to speak of. Cringing with horror, he anticipated the worst.

Looking to his left, he observed a sign that read "Kittery" with an arrow that pointed up. His heart flooded with dread; it was suddenly impossible for him to breathe. Maybe it was just the sand stuck to the inside of his lungs, or maybe it was the fact that thousands of innocent people were about to die. Just then, Karl noticed a strangely placed lever around a hundred yards away from the sign.

It must be a switch to change the train's course of direction, he thought to himself.

Burning with hope, he tried to stand on his feet but simply did not have the strength. Crashing back down to earth, a terrible sadness caused his face to clam up with angst. He desperately and neurotically tossed the crowbar in the general direction of the switch; it obviously did not reach. Karl lay on his back and closed

217

his eyes, finally admitting defeat. The train rolled on as it carried out its impending sentence of doom.

"Sir, we have visuals to suggest there may be a slight problem," a hooded man reported to his boss.

"And what would that be?"

"The train's course changed just now. You're going to have to see this to believe it . . . " he mumbled.

The other Council members that were in The Man's private chamber nervously fidgeted around the room.

"Stay still, you fools! Camera twenty-three feed into monitor three."

A still photograph of the back end of a protruding bulldozer was revealed, inadvertently flipping the switch. The Man, who remained as collected as usual, stood up and concentrated with the vast majority of his brain. He planned on using someone onboard to access a hidden emergency break that was underneath the main control panel. Certainly he was within range for his thoughts to reach theirs; he picked up only one mind. For some reason, he could not force the individual to move from their current location; they were pinned down by something that he didn't have time to determine. After protesting and screaming endlessly, now knowing full well what was about to happen, Kutu took a deep breath.

The Man turned to his colleagues with an expressionless face.

"Failures. You were all failures to me."

Hundreds of tons of burning steel fragmented into the Council Headquarters' docking area as the train rammed into the wall at the rear end of the entry tunnel. The cars pilled up, one on top of the other, and with the addition of each car to the stack, the raging collision intensified. Due to the extreme temperature, the explosives finally detonated and spewed debris clear through every inch of the compound. The Man and his Council associates were instantly obliterated.

The only person that would have a smile on his sand-bitten

face in the desert tonight would be Karl; mainly because everyone else had just been vaporized. An awe-inspiring cloud of dirt ironically delivered new hope that perhaps this was the beginning of the end of Council neutrality. Karl ran his fingers through his hair and thanked God for the first miracle he'd ever witnessed.

48

She Screams in Silence

They could feel the cameras' cold electronic eyes stalking their every move. Jacob and Marlana were on national television again. The couple, very content, held hands and quietly rested against one another as supporters from both factions impatiently awaited a response. In the middle of the nation's only neutral town, they sat, admiring the temporary sanity.

Although most citizens were naturally a tad agitated standing side by side with the enemy, the law allowed tranquillity, as long as it was for a brief duration of time. Abyss had always functioned as the meeting place for the sides to discuss a time and place for various wars to be fought. Conveniently located in between Boston and Kittery, fifty miles away from either city, it worked well as a common ground. If something did go wrong, the Council was previously located close by; about twenty-five miles north. Aside from the Brotherhood no one else dared to sleep overnight in the smoldering wasteland of a desert. Tribes of rogues did settle long ago, but they were forced, due to sandstorms and chemical rain, to move further south, closer to the ghettos surrounding the Imperial capitol of Despair.

The Empress' orders rang in their ears like the menacing caw of a raven. Unable to come to a decision, they observed the couple. Some were on the verge of returning to their traditional ways, and others secretly desired nothing more than a long-sought-after peace. Change was in the air; along with bits and pieces of smoldering debris from an explosion in the desert. Granted, the crowd chose not to openly comment on the situation, it was understood what had just happened. The people were taking a forceful stand, despite the severity of consequences.

"Everyone is sick of fighting," Marlana said. "And as you can all see, the people that gather around you are not your real enemies."

She fixed her hair and placed her head on Jacob's shoulder.

"They'll be here to pick us up real soon."

"Coming to the town square was a good idea; everyone is too confused to start any trouble. We need to use this!"

Marlana stood up and began to preach her beliefs, remembering what Atkins had told her.

"See what it's like not to kill each other? We can actually stand here and talk. Let's keep things this way. There's nothing the Council can do if we all just stand around and do nothing!" she exclaimed.

A few people nodded their heads in agreement. As she spoke, her message was broadcasted with the potential for every citizen to hear her plea.

"Why is everyone looking at us?"

"We're famous now, Jacob, and I can't say that I don't like it. It's time we do something. Now that we have the chance."

"Marlana, honey, I know how hard this Game thing can be. I want it to end as well, but the Empire, it . . . "

His speech faded and Jacob's eyes lowered to the ground. She knew that he was never going to give in. Hardheadedness was a quality that all the men in her life seemed to possess. Thinking back to what she vowed to do, her voice grew raspy. Blocking any conflicting thoughts from her mind, she sat back down.

"That's all I can ask of you people."

Jacob appeared relieved that she finally stopped the verbal onslaught.

"Marlana, I just want you to know that I love you. More than ever. We've been through more together in just a few years than some people have in their whole lives."

"I know, honey. We've been tested. And we passed."

An easy feeling passed over her face and Marlana glowed with contentment.

"No matter the outcome, we still have each other."

Whether she was distracted by the war or not, Marlana was taken by Jacob's comments and the shadow of their brief arguing had passed.

"You're right, Marle. No matter what you decide to do, I'll be here for you," he said with a warm smile.

An intimate embrace may not have been a good enough conclusion for the nation's spectators. The uneasy question of "what now?" lingered on. Marlana touched Jacob's hand and kissed him. When she had opened her eyes she paid close attention to a sudden jerking from within the crowd.

Manfred harshly limped in front of the couple. Never removing his eyes from Jacob, his usual villainous motif was gone and replaced by a shell of his former self. An endless sea of agony filled his pupils with an almost sickening emptiness. Manfred reminded Marlana of a child that had lost a parent. There was something about him that was sad, yet more intimidating than she could stand for. His hand slowly wrapped around *Kaiser's Revenge. So this is why the Council never shut off the cameras.* It's what everyone had come to see. The Union rescue team arrived and pushed their way through the crowd. One of the soldiers handed Jacob the Council-issued machete that he had acquired over one year ago. Manfred slowly unsheathed *Kaiser's Revenge* and uncharacteristically did not utter a single word. He simply took two perfectly timed steps forward. Standing up, Jacob glanced in the direction of his motivation and kissed her on the cheek. Much like a boxing match, each man stood in their respective corner until the proverbial bell had rung.

As much as his injuries plagued him, Jacob forcibly sucked up the pain and viciously swung. Manfred deflected the attack, closed his eyes from pure exhaustion, and attempted to stab his opponent in the midsection. Clubbing Manfred's head with the hilt, he collapsed and landed on his back. Protecting his torso by grabbing Jacob's free arm and using his body weight to catch him off balance, Manfred kicked him in the ribs, and rolled over on his stomach. He then proceeded to reach his feet, but Jacob had charged and sent him back to the ground. Manfred placed his thumb in his Jacob's left eye and squeezed until the two willingly separated themselves. By now, Marlana was eyeing a pistol that was strapped to an Imperial soldier's boot.

Manfred arrogantly turned his back on the fight and walked to a storage shed that held landscaping supplies. Opening the door, he then pulled a can of gasoline. Turning the orange container upside-down he observed as liquid poured down the blade of *Kaiser's Revenge.* He was suspiciously cautious of overspill.

Not realizing what was going on due to the sheer amount of adrenaline pumping through his veins, Jacob approached his rival without much thought. Delivering an evil message through a well-placed smile of sadism, Manfred removed his cigarette lighter and ignited the sword. Abruptly swinging at Jacob, who naturally blocked the advancement, Manfred pushed forward as steel slid against steel. Gasoline flowed onto Jacob and flames spread to his sleeve. Manfred proceeded to stomp on his ribs and back while Jacob thrashed on the ground, desperately attempting to put out the fire.

Taking a page from Manfred's book, he slugged Agent Vega where the sun doesn't shine. Both men struggled for survival as they let go of their weapons and tried to strangle the life from one another with their bare hands. Breathing heavily, they neared exhaustion.

Half of Manfred's attacks blatantly missed. His muscles were practically frozen from soreness. Blood poured from his nose and leaked into his mouth; he spit some in Jacob's face. Speaking of Jacob's face, his right eye was so swollen and caked over with blood, he had lost peripheral vision. Manfred, capitalizing on this, psychotically struck him in the side of the head, and then collapsed from pure fatigue. Both men lay as if lifeless; the crowd, almost mimicking the combatants, grew silent with anticipation.

Jacob was first to regain consciousness. Due to his aching, pounding head, Manfred's hearing was greatly impaired. While his eyes were temporarily closed he did not hear the approaching forearm as it cracked his jaw, spilling a small ocean of blood. Jacob picked up his sword on the second attempt; a slippery coating of blood prohibited a firm grip.

Crawling on top of Manfred, he raised the Council's machete, blade pointing to the ground, over his head. Thinking fast, Manfred leaned over and seized *Kaiser's Revenge*. Swinging to form a semi-circle that was nearing Jacob's body, the following two seconds seemed like days. Jacob, using all of his might to push his blade downward, slightly turned his head to catch a glimpse of Marlana, who was now aiming a stolen pistol at Manfred. A sudden burst of love for his fiancée rang through his body, overtaking even his most painful wounds. The man in black's eyes burned a hole through Jacob's forehead; he prayed to God that his blade would reach his adversary before he, himself, met his cold-blooded end.

Smack in the middle of his would-be hour of darkness, an event was on the verge of preventing the almost inevitable slaying of Marlana's favorite villain. A single bullet bore its way through Jacob's torso and created a sickening exit-wound, spraying blood onto Manfred's face. He cringed backward in excruciating pain while Manfred released his grasp on *Kaiser's Revenge* and scurried along the dirt floor behind a protective wall of bystanders.

Two additional gunshots pierced Marlana's inner ear. A thin line of blood oozed down the side of her neck. She took an unwilling step forward and dropped the firearm. Experiencing a surreal moment of clarity, Jacob came to the realization that the love of his life placed three small hunks of lead into his body. Jacob fell down and landed on his right side; he closed his eyes and impatiently waited for his unwanted life to filter into nothingness. As the shadow of death was passing over his body, Jacob acknowledged that his heart had died moments ago. He did not know her justifications, and he simply didn't have the time left to think about them either. Perhaps content with what he once had, Jacob allowed himself to slip away.

As though he had witnessed the birth, life, and death of a god, Manfred wearily ran his fingers through his hair and stumbled out from his hiding place. Opening his mouth to speak, he decided that words could not express his emotions and said nothing. Extending his hand to Marlana, he waited for some kind of a response. She turned her back to him and closed her eyes.

It was the only way. Marlana thought back to her conversations with Jacob and recalled the countless times that he vowed to fight this war. The citizens had witnessed what should happen to anyone that refused to lay down their weapons and unite. This was her life-ending sacrifice; Jacob wasn't the only one to die. Marlana's brain twisted and turned in order to try and deal with the stone cold facts. Upon witnessing the blank expression on Marlana's face, an Imperial soldier leaned toward his associate and whispered into his ear.

"If she was willing to kill the guy she loved, to prove a point, to end The Game, it should be easy for the rest of us to do what we have to."

After hearing those words, the other man reluctantly turned to a Union soldier and nodded his head as a sign of neutrality. The Council nationally broadcasted the entire chain of events, including all conversation. Their once prominent plan of manipulation had backfired. Instead of one man killing the other and furthering the war, Marlana proved to the world that there did not need to be a war. She had delivered a message to all those that promote The Game: you will be suppressed, no matter the circumstance. They were witnessing the dawn of a revolution, and now that the cards were played, it was only a matter of time before the two sides joined forces to face a greater evil.

"What now?" a citizen asked.

"Let's go to the core. They can't stop us all. We'll *make* them give us a cure to the poison," he said, turning his body as he spoke to the crowd.

"Yeah, let's go."

"Fuck the Council and their bullshit!"

"There are more of us than there are of them!"

"Down with the Council!"

Manfred had about one million questions that meshed together and formed one giant ball of garbage within his head. She had used him to portray a message to the public. Lowering his head, Manfred grew weary from combat, and took a moment to reflect on Marlana. Understanding that he could never have her for whatever reason she created next, he did feel awfully grateful that she didn't kill him when she had the chance. If she did, however, it would have weakened her cause and illustrated disunity amongst the sides. She had to let him be. The only way for her to achieve the impossible was to remove a member of her own faction that did not spit in the face of *their* rules.

Half of him yearned to place a hand on Marlana's shoulder and comfort her from a self-inflicted broken heart, but he knew better. The newly born hero screamed inside her head until her brain boiled and her guts turned rotten. A single tear escaped the prison that was her body and slid down her colorless face. Marlana twitched for someone to hold her, but she had murdered the man she loved and could not bring him back no matter how much remorse seeped from her bleeding heart.

And with the revelation that there was nothing left for him to accomplish, Manfred lit a cigarette and began to limp away, gently pushing people from his path. He didn't know where he was going; he just walked. For reasons that weren't entirely clear to him, he didn't feel like the bad guy any longer. Taking an extended drag from his cigarette, Manfred decided to find a bar that would serve a good martini.